# The Adventures of Charlee Rae and Billy True

Bedside Books
An imprint of American Book Publishing
5442 So. 900 East, #146
Salt Lake City, UT 84117-7204
www.american-book.com

Printed in the United States of America on acid-free paper.

The Adventures of Charlee Rae and Billy True
Designed by Andriy Yankovskyy, design@american-book.com

**Publisher's Note:** This is a work of fiction. Names, characters, places, and incidents either are the product of the author's imagination, or are used fictitiously, and any resemblance to actual persons, living or dead, events, or locales is entirely coincidental.

ISBN-13: 978-1-58982-448-5
ISBN-10: 1-58982-448-2

Schuetz, Jack L.
    The Adventures of Charlee Rae and Billy True

*Special Sales*
These books are available at special discounts for bulk purchases. Special editions, including personalized covers, excerpts of existing books, and corporate imprints, can be created in large quantities for special needs. For more information e-mail info@american-book.com.

# The Adventures of Charlee Rae and Billy True

**Jack L. Schuetz**

I dedicate this book to my family: my wife, Lavonne, for years of caring and support; my children: Mike, Kara, Todd, and Amy; and, especially, my grandchildren: D.J., Jack, and Piper. They all give me great pleasure and delight.

I am grateful for the assistance of Tom McGuigan of the North Gila Historical Society in Payson, Arizona.

Geoffrey Lewis

# The Adventures of Charlee Ray and Billy True

## Foreword by Geoffrey Lewis

Just to give you a little background about myself and how I came to love this story – as I am sure you will too – about heroes and heroines, good guys and bad guys.

I was born in New Jersey where I prowled the woods for ten years, and then moved to the high desert of California and the higher mountains that sat on the horizon. I prowled this landscape too and went to high school and college here in the empty west. I grew up with cowboys; I learned their language and got in fist fights – just for fun.

The first movie I ever made was called "The Culpepper Cattle Company," which has since become known as the "quintessential cattle-drive movie." After that movie, I went on to be in a bunch of westerns. I got to be a pretty good rider and a fast gun, though not a very good roper. I ended up with ten horses in my backyard and a pack of stories that all the old leather-headed cowboys used to tell me.

Now, I'm not going to sit here and unravel this marvelous story for you – you can do that and it's quite a ride – but I want to tell you a couple of things because I told Jack I would, and it is my pleasure.

There are different ways for information to be passed along from one person to another, but probably the most entertaining way is to tell a story. Stories are special because they move along - they start at one place and end up another. On the ride you discover all kinds of things and you share in the lives of people you will come to know as real-life characters and life-long friends. In a way, you get to live extra lives.

Jack has very skillfully put together a story with rich emotions and great substance. It rolls along naturally, with surprises, wonderfully colorful people and of course, real-life adventures. There are sure to be ideas you can use in your own life. At times it will get harrowing; it will make you mad, make you laugh, make you happy, bring realizations, and you might even fall in love. It's a *real* story.

You're going to find some of yourself in Charlee or Billy, maybe even Charlee's ma, Rudd Leland, or any one of the many well-drawn characters. I think most of all, you are going to enjoy the world Jack has created for us, and probably, you will read it more than once. Have a good time.

# Map

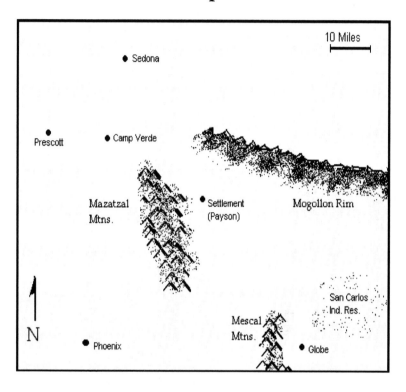

10 Miles

Sedona

Prescott

Camp Verde

Mazatzal
Mtns.

Settlement
(Payson)

Mogollon Rim

San Carlos
Ind. Res.

Mescal
Mtns.

N

Phoenix

Globe

# Introduction to the Reader

The aftermath of the Civil War produced a flow of people westward. The Verde Valley and Tonto Basin of Arizona were rich with rivers and accompanying fertile bottomland, water, and game. In this area, a family could live, work, and prosper. Our story is situated in this land.

The region hosted danger as well. The native people, or Indians, displaced by settlers and mistreated by the United States government, sometimes became hostile. Outlaws took advantage of the limited influence of the law. Bandits raided wagon trains, towns, and ranches.

In 1863, Congress separated the Arizona territory from New Mexico. Gold and silver mining drew more people to the area. Federal troops were committed in 1863 with two companies of California volunteers' cavalry. The First Infantry was located at Fort Whipple in the Prescott area. This provided some security from Indian raids and helped open up settlement.

The settlement where Charlee Rae and Billy True live is located at the site of present-day Payson, Arizona. The area had less law and was remote from larger settlements, like Camp Verde and Cottonwood. This story is a testament to the courage and resilience of pioneers in this area. Charlee and Billy, and their friends and family, reflect the people who developed the territory. They are models of these pioneers.

I created Charlee Rae and Billy True as exceptional people. They surpass others in the quality of their efforts to live on this wild frontier. Although the characters lived first in my imagination, the places and historical events are as true as I could make them. I traveled with my wife to Payson in the winter of 2006 and stood where Billy and Charlee would have stood. I set the story in the years between 1860 and 1880 because it was a time of rapid change, and as their world changes around them, Charlee Rae and Billy True grow up and change, too. They learn about themselves, tackle challenges, make mistakes, and discover friendship and love. Some things have not changed in the past century.

Jack L. Schuetz
Bakersfield, California

# Chapter 1: The Attack on Arrow

Sweat ran down Billy's suntanned face as he followed a faint trail where he had been tracking deer. He was close, and shifted his Sharps to a ready position. His senses were acutely directed to the sounds, smells, and view of his surroundings.

A vague, distant sound interrupted this intensity and caused him to drop to one knee to listen and study the environment around him. Billy listened more intently to the sounds around him.

There it was, faraway, a sound drifting over the hills and canyons around him. Billy left the deer trail and climbed to the top of a small mesa. The sound came again, this time more clearly. He was startled by the realization that the faint sounds were repeated gunfire.

Billy reasoned the gunfire was not from the guns of hunters or target practice—there was no pattern. This was a gunfight. Billy surmised the shots were coming from the north. What was over there? The only thing he could recall was the Arrow Ranch, two miles away.

Bolting back to where he had tied his horse, Billy slid the

Sharps into the scabbard and swung up into the saddle. Calculating his route as he rode, he weaved through rock clusters and clumps of brush. Billy found a familiar trail that he knew would lead toward Arrow Ranch. The sounds were closer.

Billy approached the ranch, keeping below the skyline to avoid being seen. He tied off his horse, pulled the Sharps from the scabbard, and moved toward the ranch house. He crawled up to the crest of a hogback that drifted above the Arrow Ranch. Intruders had surrounded the house where the Darrow family was making a stand.

Billy had spent many days at the ranch helping Willard Darrow with various odd jobs. His scouting, tracking, hunting, and general ranch skills made Billy an asset for the Darrows, a family with one daughter and no sons.

Of particular concern for Billy was his friend Charlee Rae Darrow. She had grown up on the ranch and was a valuable member of the ranch corps. Billy had taught her to shoot with a handgun and rifle the previous summer. He wondered if she were returning fire now.

Billy viewed the scene, counting five intruders—two in back and three in the front of the house. The intruders' horses—a gray, white, pinto, black, and a sorrel—were tied off behind the barn. He moved to the crest of the hogback, working through the mesquite for cover.

Billy was about two hundred yards from the house. From the sound of the gunfire, there seemed to be two or three defenders in the house. If Billy could provide crossfire against the intruders, it might make them withdraw.

Billy had his .50 caliber Sharps with him, his favorite gun for hunting deer and larger game. The breech loading was slow, but the gun had good range. If he could take down an intruder, it might discourage the rest. He adjusted his sites at two hundred yards and rested the gun on a steady cross branch of the mesquite. His code was not to kill unless absolutely necessary.

Billy aimed at the legs of the closest man. He squeezed the trigger, and the report was followed by the screams of the man. The impact of the round took the man's legs out from under him and he sprawled out in view of the others. Billy immediately emptied his .44 Colt revolver at the intruders. The gun would not be effective at that range, but created a hectic scene around the house. Sensing what was happening, the people in the house increased their fire. The intruders, imagining they were outnumbered and flanked, took to their horses and fled down the valley, heading for the many mountain canyons awaiting them.

Billy retreated back to where he had tied his horse to a small tree. After reloading his guns he mounted and rode the ridge to make sure the fleeing riders had cleared the area and not doubled back. He scanned the area with his field glass and saw dust swirls far down the valley on a trail leading to the breaks below the mountains.

Billy sat on his horse for some time, studying the ground taken by the intruders. His mind wandered to the thought of Charlee Rae. He imagined her safe, and a slight smile crossed his face. He dropped into the valley and headed for Arrow. Following the tree line, Billy rode around the clearing, making sure there were no intruders left, dead or alive. The one he had hit must have been thrown on a horse to retreat with the others.

Approaching the house, Billy called out, "You can come out now. This is Billy True. The intruders are all gone toward the mountains."

Willard Darrow came out first, cradling his Winchester rifle in his arms. He smiled as he recognized Billy standing beside his horse.

"Well, Hoss," Willard barked, "you're sure a welcome sight. Those men came upon us at daybreak. I don't know what they wanted; we do keep large amounts of cash here to pay our hands and buy supplies."

From the house came Bertha, Willard's wife. Close behind appeared Charlee Rae. She ran to Billy, jumped up, swinging her arms around his neck, and gave him a kiss on the cheek. Surprised, Billy lifted her down and blushingly said, "Charlee Rae, you stop that. It's not fitting."

"Billy True, I've known you for years. A little peck is appropriate." She looked at him from under lowered eyelids. "You're like a brother."

Bertha interrupted the awkward moment by asking Billy if he could stay for dinner. Billy turned to Bertha and pointed at his clothes. "Thank you, ma'am, but these buckskins are a little ripe. I've been riding hard and am a little sweaty."

Bertha, used to ranch smells, waved a hand and said, "Son, after what you did here today, a little smell from your buckskins is no issue."

"It doesn't bother me at all," Charlee chimed. That twinkle was in her eyes again and Billy blushed.

"Let's wash up, Hoss," Willard said in his familiar voice. The name Hoss had recently been given to Billy by the Arrow hands because he was big for seventeen. He had thrown many cowboys in friendly wrestling matches.

The washbasins were stationed beside the raised water tank where shower nozzles were mounted inside the tank's skirts.

Willard and Billy stripped off their shirts and began

soaping and rinsing. Charlee Rae appeared from the house with a large bucket of hot water. "You fellas like to have some hot water?"

Willard was surprised and pleased to wash with hot water. Billy, however, was self-conscious and not used to a girl coming up on him without his shirt on. After a clumsy moment Charlie retreated back to the house as Bertha beckoned her. Bertha was aware of her daughter's interest in Billy. She appreciated Billy's efforts to keep Charlee Rae in a proper place and distance in their relationship.

Bertha set a bountiful table, consistent with her reputation. Charlee was careful to point out her own contributions to the dinner so Billy would notice. She heaped servings of mashed potatoes and gravy on his plate. Billy watched her agile hands.

"Hoss, what do you think about these intruders?" Willard asked as he hailed Billy's attention from across the table.

Billy pondered and replied, "This could be a gang coming out of the breaks below the Rim. It could be part of Rudd Leland's bunch."

Rudd Leland had raided the Arizona territory for years. He was part White Mountain Apache and part Anglo. He moved easily through both worlds causing trouble. Billy had planted a rifle bullet in Rudd's leg in '73 while riding with a cavalry troop trying to capture the outlaw. He had sworn he would be more thorough next time.

Willard stretched and reached for his pipe. Charlee Rae frowned and said, "Dad, Mom doesn't want you to smoke that pipe in the house."

Bertha reacted instantly. "True, Charlee Rae, but I will correct your father."

Undaunted, Charlee retreated from the table with a load of dishes. The men moved to the porch that breasted the house.

Willard expressed concern over the security of the ranch as he puffed at his pipe.

"I will have to bring some riders back closer to the house," he told Billy. "I can't risk leaving the women open to this kind of attack." He looked at the young man. "Billy, could I hire you to scout the breaks to make sure this bunch has moved back into the mountains?"

Billy looked at Bertha and Charlee in the doorway and saw anguish on their faces. He was thoughtful for a moment. "I promised some miners I would get a deer for them," he said. "That's what I was doing when I heard this ruckus. I'll get a fresh horse and outfit with supplies for a few days."

Billy edged toward the porch steps. It was a six-mile ride to the settlement, and it would take some time to get a deer to the miner's camp. Billy rested his Sharps in the scabbard and cinched up his saddle.

"I'll not likely see you for a few days," Billy commented as he swung up on his horse.

Willard called to Billy, "There is a stand of deer up the draw above the house. You might try there first. Be careful, Hoss. Don't take chances with these raiders."

Bertha and Charlee came out of the house to add their own conditions. Charlee Rae called out, "Billy, you come back to me as soon as you finish Dad's business."

Billy waved and rode off toward the draw above the house. Within two hours, Billy had shot and field-dressed a deer, and was on his way to the mining camp. The camps were of interest to Billy because he had part interest in two of the mines. He liked to visit the camps, discuss progress, and hear stories about the miners' pasts.

# Chapter 2: The Scout for Arrow

Billy was supplied for five days of dry, cold camp. He would not risk fires from camp—his work would require stealth and cunning and caution.

He had been following the outer ranges of Arrow looking for signs of intruders. He moved in a serpentine pattern to watch his back trail and to systematically cover more ground.

Stopping periodically, Billy scanned the mountains and breaks around him. His glass gave him a vantage point in searching the brows of the mountains and the many ravines of the breaks. He had encountered old tracks of Indians and shod horse tracks. He studied these for peculiar signs and to determine when they were made. The possibility of Rudd Leland being around concerned Billy.

On one of his zigzag patterns, Billy caught a glimpse of a rider shadowing his trail. He doubled back and stood down from his horse. He posted himself where the rider would come under his gun before he realized Billy was there.

As the rider came into view, Billy determined he was rigged like a cowhand. As the rider approached, Billy recognized the person as Jim Ream, an Arrow hand. Billy hailed him and approached the startled rider.

"If I had intended you harm, you'd be dead. What are you doing way up here, Jim?"

Ream, still a little surprised, replied, "I saw your tracks and thought I would check."

Billy explained about the raid on Arrow and that the hands were being called in closer to the ranch house.

"What are you doing up here?" Ream asked.

Billy described his job and suggested that Jim head back the same way he had come, and to keep a cold camp until he reached the ranch house.

"Why didn't the boss send some of the older men?" Ream blurted.

Billy took a deep breath. "You'll have to take it up with him when you get back." As he strode toward his horse, Billy tossed over his shoulder, "You might watch for signs of the intruders. I haven't crossed their trail yet. They are probably northwest of us. I suggest you stay on the trail you left."

Jim Ream was not impressed with the suggestions of a seventeen-year-old boy and planned to feign his back trail and veer to the northwest. He figured he would stand well with Willard Darrow if he could upstage Billy True on his scouting duties.

Billy decided to find a vantage point to scan the country to the northwest. He had been out three days and his horse needed rest, pasture, and grain. He would cut this day short.

Billy's vantage point looked out on mountain ridges shaped like tabernacles. The breaks settled in below the mountains, giving way to small valleys and soft meadows. There was an active brook nearby for water and a patch of grass for graze.

Billy settled in for the night, positioning his saddle and blanket to cradle his tired body. His eyes browsed the surrounding country, ever watchful. His mind drifted to the Arrow Ranch. A fleeting thought of Charlee Rae came to Billy, her triumphant eyes, alive and knowing, sharing a look of silent communication.

Bertha had been up for some time, helping the ranch cook get supplies from the cellar. Charlee Rae started the coffee. Willard came in from chores and hugged Charlee playfully. She responded with a couched complaint but loved every minute of it. Bertha came in and set out the breakfast makings of ham, eggs, and biscuits. She and Charlee worked as a team to ready the kitchen for the day.

Charlee moved to the window on the east, fixed her eyes on the distant mountains, and said, "I wonder where Billy is now?" She turned to face her father. "You shouldn't send him out on this kind of job alone. What will he do if he runs into the gang that hit us?"

Willard shifted his weight in his chair. He spoke cautiously as if preparing an unwanted discussion. "Charlee, Billy is the best scout in these parts. This job calls for stealth and cunning. One man, like Billy, can move relatively undetected. He won't get into a skirmish unless absolutely necessary. If he does, those on the other end will feel the mark of that Winchester rifle of his."

Charlee looked away without responding. She knew when it was not wise to push an issue with her dad.

After breakfast Bertha and Charlee faced the trials of the workday in the kitchen, although Charlee was going to ride out to check some range with Willard in the afternoon.

"Mom, what do you think about my concern about

Billy?" Charlee asked as she was clearing the table. Bertha hesitated, choosing her words carefully.

"We are all concerned about Billy being out there, particularly when this frontier has been troubled by unrest. Your dad is very worried about Billy. He probably wished he had not sent him. Don't continue to badger him."

Charlee shook her head. "Then why doesn't Dad send out some riders to find and help Billy?" Charlee whispered.

"It is not for you or me to say. Dad gave a lot of thought to this. Let's talk about something else now," Bertha replied as she took Charlee by the shoulders and gazed into her eyes.

Small talk flowed in the kitchen for most of the morning. Bertha was creating some of her famous apple pies, enough for the family and hands. Charlee was peeling potatoes and imagining a life with Billy. Suddenly she twirled a potato peel over her head like a lasso. "Mom!" she announced with glee, "I'm not just a kid anymore. I'll be a woman. I can get married!"

Bertha gestured with a fork over her pies. "Not just yet, little lady—there's more to growing up than blossoming out and growing taller."

"There are girls on the frontier my age already married. I'm sixteen now!"

"What do you want out of life, Charlee?" her mother asked. "Will it be drudgery and the unhappiness of a lost childhood?"

"No, I want to be an accomplished ranch wife, like you have taught me. I'm a good ranch hand like Dad has shown me. I don't want to just live on a ranch, I want to run it. I want to be involved in the decisions. Dad told me this ranch would be mine when it's time. I plan to run it."

Bertha was not surprised by Charlee's comments; her body

had not outstripped her mind. The name Charlee Rae was taken from two challenging characters known by Bertha and Willard. They had wished for a personality just like Charlee.

Before Bertha could fully fathom these issues, Charlee commented, "Mom, what I want more than anything is Billy."

Bertha gasped and dropped a pan in the sink. She knew Charlee was fond of Billy and had suspected it might go this way someday, but not so soon.

"Charlee," the girl's mother said firmly, "Billy is a young man. He is not ready for the challenge you would present to him. Give him time to mature."

"He is more of a man now than those I see around here," Charlee argued. "Where is he now? He's out on the range doing work that only he could be trusted with."

Bertha addressed Charlee with concentration. "Billy was trained for this work, mostly by the Apaches, before he came to live with the Murphys. He has learned ranch skills from your father on this ranch."

Bertha braced herself for Charlee's response; it didn't come. Bertha seized the moment.

"Charlee, Billy is a remarkable person blessed with physical power and keen intuition. He will grow into an outstanding man, but maybe he's not necessarily for you."

Charlee shifted her position to be straight on to Bertha. "Mom," she said, her tone softer, "it isn't fair. I see those girls in the settlement giggling and smiling at him. They don't plan to wait around until Billy matures to attract him. You say I must wait, but will he wait for me? I have a right to let him know how I feel, and that I want him with me on Arrow, and have a family."

"He may not want to be a rancher," Bertha said calmly.

"You have to give him a chance to breathe or you may drive him away."

Charlee pondered Bertha's statement. Then her mood shifted like a stormy sky. "I will tell him," Charlee announced, twirling around with a dishtowel in her hand, "when and how I don't know."

Bertha took the moment to curb the discussion. Taking the dishtowel from her daughter's hand, she said, "We will discuss this more later."

Charlee seemed to accept the respite and joined her mother with other tasks.

The next morning Billy fixed his eyes on the horizon at the start of the new day. He realized each day must be lived with care in his chancy work. He had jerky and some of Mom Murphy's biscuits for breakfast. With his glass he scanned the panorama around him, plotted his route, and registered possible areas that would make him vulnerable.

He would work to the northwest, keeping the higher mountains on his right and the breaks below and to the left, keeping the zigzag pattern as he scouted.

He headed northwest following the furrow of an old trail. A dark hairline against the mountain on the right indicated a main trail winding lazily along the incline. The trail switched backed down the mountain, coming close to his position. Stopping to let his horse blow, Billy viewed the surrounding country, amazed at its beauty and expanse.

Suddenly, a faint sound drew Billy's attention to the trail below and ahead of him. He settled his horse in a nearby spruce patch. Pulling his Winchester from its scabbard, he climbed to a vantage point. The main trail turned on a switchback about fifty yards in front of him. He went to a kneeling position and peered over the edge of the knoll.

Anxiety and excitement ranged through his body as he spotted seven men on horseback. They were leading two pack mules and a horse. They were out about two hundred yards and closing on his position as they followed the trail. With his glass Billy studied the string. The men were well armed and not outfitted like trappers or hunters. The horse being led was the black Jim Ream had been riding—the gear was still there. One man was dangling a leg from his stirrup as if injured. Billy noticed a pinto and white similar to the horses he had seen at the Arrow Ranch.

Is this the bunch that attacked Arrow? There were only five at Arrow. Two could have been held back to manage the stock. Why were they here? They should have made better time. They could have holed up to hide and rest the wounded man. They would have had to kill Jim to get his horse.

Shoot to wound a couple and knock down some horses or shoot to kill? Billy wondered to himself. He killed only when necessary.

Convinced these were the raiders, Billy decided they must suffer some casualties to pay for damage to the ranch and for killing Jim. For his own safety he needed to knock down as many men as he could. He could force them up the trail, away from him, and over the mountain. If some were killed, that would be the luck of it.

Billy waited until the last two men were abreast of him on the switchback. The shooting would force the men up the trail and not back down. If some got down the trail, Billy could be caught in crossfire. Billy's first volley knocked the last two riders off their horses. He swung his rifle and raked the column with rapid gunfire. One man slumped and a horse went down. Two men in the front dismounted, kneeled, and returned fire on Billy's position. Billy rotated his body to face the threat and exchanged fire for a few moments.

Suddenly a stinging pain hit his left forearm and shoulder. Billy had been hit. The two men mounted and the remainder of the column fled up the trail. Billy fired shots to the sides of the trail to keep the men in hot retreat.

When the men were well out of range and moving away, Billy surveyed the scene. Most of the animals had followed the string up the mountain. The two mules had drifted away, one down the trail and near Billy's position. Using the glass he watched the remainder of the men still moving up the mountain.

The pain in his arm and shoulder was increasing. He found that no bones had been broken, and that he could move his arm and shoulder. He got some bandages from his saddlebags and put compression packs on his wounds to stop the bleeding. Billy would have to get back to the ranch as soon as possible.

Billy needed to find Jim, bury him, or take him back to the ranch. He climbed back to the trail to find the mule that had drifted down. The mule was standing about fifty yards down and to the side of the trail. Billy went to his horse and led it toward the mule, gently whistling to soothe the animal. The mule hesitated and walked toward Billy. Billy loosened and threw the pack off the animal. He took the canvas pack cover from the pile and secured a lead rope to the mule's halter.

Stowing the canvas on his horse, Billy walked down the trail, backtracking the intruders. He stopped periodically to check if the intruders had turned back. He was fearful he would find Jim's body.

The intruders' trail was easy to follow, and Billy made good time. In a cluster of spruce Billy found Jim Ream. The cowboy had camped and apparently had been caught by surprise. There was no sign of a fight, he was not tied, and his throat had been cut—a hard way to die. Billy felt a lump in his throat as he thought of what Jim had gone through. The raiders had stolen Jim's clothes and he lay naked. Billy wrapped the body in the pack canvas and tied it on the mule. He reasoned he was about a day and a half away, heading straight to the ranch.

The evening of the next day Billy was two miles from the ranch when he encountered a hand. He told the rider to go ahead and warn the Darrows he was coming in.

"Ask them to keep the women, particularly Charlee, away because Jim is naked and getting a little ripe in this warm weather."

The Darrows were getting ready for dinner when the rider came galloping in. Willard went out to meet him and get the report. Charlee and Bertha were waiting to hear what the ruckus was. Willard told them. "Billy's coming in bringing Jim Ream's body. Please stay back because it won't be a pretty sight."

Billy rode in leading the mule. He stopped at the barn and met Willard and some hands. He said quietly, "Jim's naked and has his throat cut. He needs to go under soon."

Willard asked the hands to take care of Ream's body and stable the animals. Willard and Billy walked toward the house. Billy, weakened by his wounds and the long ride, staggered a little. Willard stopped to look Billy over.

"My gosh, Hoss, you've been wounded." He yelled to the house, "Bertha, Billy's been hit, get a place ready."

Willard held Billy's injured arm and assisted him toward the house.

Charlee and Bertha had been readying the cot and preparing

the bandages made from strips of old cotton cloth. Billy came in and insisted on sitting at the table instead of the cot.

Charlee had been composed to this point, but seeing Billy in pain and bleeding was more than she could bear. Tears welled up in her eyes and she whispered through her sobs, "Billy, does it hurt bad? I'm sorry."

Bertha told Charlee to get some hot water and clean bandages. Bertha cut the buckskin shirt off Billy to examine the wounds. The forearm wound was deep but clean—a good compress would help. The shoulder gave them more concern. The bullet was still inside and protruded under the skin in the back.

"The bullet has to come out," Bertha directed. "We need to take Billy to Doc Pierce or have him come out here. Let's take him into town in the buckboard. The Murphys need to be told as soon as we hit town."

While the buckboard was being readied, Bertha gave Billy one of Willard's shirts to put on. She asked, "Billy, do you want anything?"

"A cup of coffee and some of those biscuits would be good," Billy joked.

Charlee assisted Billy with the shirt. "Billy," she said, "you have to stop going on these scout things. I could lose you."

Billy smiled inquisitively and said nothing.

It was getting dark by the time they got Billy into town. They found the doctor in his office. Doc asked everyone to leave the room so he could examine Billy.

"Well, Hoss," he said as he approached the young man, "you finally caught one." He removed Billy's shirt carefully and mused, "Looks like you were hit while aiming your rifle. It grazed your forearm and spent in your shoulder."

After his examination, Doc commented, "No bones

involved, and mostly soft tissue, some muscle, and maybe tendons. We'll have to get the bullet out. It shouldn't be difficult since it's close to the surface in the back."

Doc gave Billy some medicine for the pain and asked him to rest while he talked to the Darrows. Doc told the Darrows about the surgery he would do. Charlee wanted to see Billy, but Doc said he would be drowsy from the medicine.

Willard Darrow went to the sheriff's office to make arrangements for Jim and to report Billy's encounter with the intruders. Sheriff Ira Brady was an itinerant officer, appointed by the government in Prescott to serve portions of the Tonto Basin.

Sheriff Brady was concerned about Billy's welfare and his fight with the gang. He was worried about the reports from the territory about gangs of marauders and bands of rogue Indians raiding small settlements and ranches.

"We may have to call the governor and ask for troops to clear the breaks and mountains where these gangs come from," Brady pondered. "If not, we will need a militia for on-call service to secure the area."

"It may come to that," Willard responded. "I haven't talked to Billy about the details of his scouting trip, how Jim was killed, or the fight he had with the gang. You can bet he left some bodies and a bunch of scared men running for their lives."

"Have you ever seen a young man like Billy?" the sheriff said as he poured a cup of coffee for Willard.

Willard gave some thought to the notion. "Young or not, I've not seen anybody like him. I wonder what he'll be like in a few years?"

"If he lives that long," sounded Ira. "He was scouting for the army when he was fifteen. That was when they were chasing Rudd Leland. He roams Apache country hunting and mining. He rides shotgun on freight wagons. The Murphys have let him go at his own pace and I'm sure they're worried."

Willard poured another cup of coffee and took a deep breath, followed by a sigh. "I probably shouldn't use him for these scouts as much as I do," he commented, "but I have the women to think about, and Billy is my best line of early warning. Charlee and Bertha scold me regularly about putting him at risk."

Bertha found Mrs. Murphy working in the kitchen and Duane Murphy in the general store. Startled by Bertha's appearance, Mildred Murphy turned pale and asked, "What's wrong? What happened to Billy?"

She was like a mother to Billy, having had him in her home for five years. He had come to live with the Murphys when his father was killed. Bertha sat down and in a calm manner explained Billy's wounds. Mildred's tears flowed like spring water. "I don't know what to do about these dangerous things," she said. "I have tried to persuade him to set up a freighting business. He has shown interest, and he can handle four-up and six-up rigs."

The room fell silent as the women gathered their thoughts. Mildred moved toward the door. "We had better go see Billy now. He'll be wondering where I am."

Bertha stayed to help Duane in the store and café while Mildred was gone.

Mildred arrived at Doc Pierce's office to find the bullet out and Doc bandaging Billy. Charlee greeted Mildred, and they both lamented their concern about Billy's dangerous work. Mildred knew Charlee had a special interest in Billy, but he never discussed her.

Mildred commented, "Billy could do a lot of things. He pans gold up in Apache country and has a large savings account. He could start ranching with the skills he learned on the Arrow." Charlee's mood brightened with this thought.

Doc Pierce came out and told Mildred and Charlee they could go in to see Billy. "I would like Billy to stay tonight and probably go home tomorrow," Doc said as he ushered the women into Billy's room.

"Mom Murphy," Billy muttered as Mildred quickly went to his side and gave him a cautious hug.

"How do you feel, son? Doc says you can come home tomorrow."

"Can't stay," Billy mumbled. "We have to scout northwest of the ranch, and they will need me to show them where to go and how to do it. There are too many tracks around not to check northwest."

"There are other people who can finish that scout," Mildred said, raising her voice to the command level.

"Now, Mom," Billy spoke quietly but intently. "You must let me use my own judgment." Billy raised himself to a sitting position. "After a night and a day, I should be ready to do a brief scout around the ranch on the northwest below the breaks. From there riders could be sent out on short trips into the breaks."

Charlee pleaded from where she stood at the bed's edge. "Listen to Mrs. Murphy. You need more rest with that wound."

Billy looked at her and smiled, "One mom is enough."

Billy got up from the bed and told Doc he was going home for some of Mom's cooking. Doc Pierce, seeing he was wasting his time, told Billy he would be by the Murphys later to check on him.

Billy and the women walked out of the office and down the street to the Murphys' place. They sat down at a café table and Billy asked if he could have something to eat.

Bertha came in from the kitchen and remarked, "My goodness, why aren't you in bed?"

Billy moaned and said, "I will be as soon as I get some of Mom's stew and a cup of coffee."

Willard found Charlee and Bertha at the Murphys' and got an update on the happenings with Billy. Charlee cornered Willard, "Dad, Billy says he needs to go back out in a couple of days to scout the northwest and show your hands how to scout the breaks. We've talked to him and he won't listen. Could you try to persuade him to stay in for a while?"

Willard reached for his pipe and fingered it. A glance from Bertha sent the pipe back into his pocket. "I'll do my best," he commented as he moved into the kitchen where Billy was eating.

Mildred was adjusting Billy's bandages. "Hoss, we need to talk," Willard muttered as he pulled up a chair. "I don't want you to go out again so soon. Give it some time. I'll send riders out to screen off the breaks. That will take care of things until we can make a plan to protect this area. Maybe we need troops or a militia. You need to be well and strong."

Billy thought the ideas made some sense and was about to agree when Bertha and Charlee came in. Willard explained his plan to them and they gave a questioning look at Billy.

Billy rose to his feet and tested his legs. He looked at Charlee. "What do you think of the plan, Charlee?" All were startled and Charlee responded, "It's a good plan." With a wry smile Billy commented, "Okay, if you say so." He calmly strolled to his room for some long overdue sleep.

Charlee was surprised. She did not know that he had

already decided to accept the plan. It was, however, Billy's way of giving her recognition and acceptance.  ·

# Chapter 3: Billy True, Apache Warrior

In 1860 Daniel True had moved to the Verde area in central Arizona to start a trading post. He brought with him a two-year-old son, Billy. His wife had died giving birth to Billy. Dan had worked at several trading posts. In response to hostility from Apache and Yavapai people in the surrounding area, a fort was built that later became a temporary Indian reservation.

When Dan arrived at Camp Verde he needed someone to help care for Billy, and he and his son occupied the building that was to be the store and living quarters. He asked the residents for recommendations. They knew of an Apache woman who had attended a missionary school in southern Arizona. Dan arranged for the woman to meet Billy. His plan was to have the woman come to the store daily to assume some domestic chores and help raise his son.

The woman arrived at the store early one morning. She was slightly stout and moved with grace. Dan greeted her warmly, relieved that she was there, and that she spoke English well. He stepped forward, hand extended in greeting.

"My name is Dan True. This is my son, Billy." The woman took Dan's hand with a gentle shake and turned immediately to the wide-eyed boy standing tall next to his dad.

"So this is Billy," she said in a gentle voice. She had soft, soothing eyes. Billy stepped forward and held out his hand, mimicking his dad. Gracefully, the woman took his hand and brought him closer. She said in a whispering voice, "You're certainly a big boy for your age." Kneeling, she cradled him gently on her arm and said, "My name is She Speaks Softly. I'm an Apache Indian." Billy, not being accustomed to a woman's attention, rested his head on her shoulder and said, "Seesoff, Seesoff." After some discussion, they determined that Seesoff was Billy's attempt to say her name, She Speaks Softly. From that time on, her name was Seesoff.

Dan discussed her duties and set the times she would work. Seesoff was gracious and pleased. She would return to her family camp daily. Her main role was to educate and train Billy.

Seesoff was from the family of the Apache chief Buckskin Hat. As Billy grew older he would visit his Indian family many times. He learned the ways of another culture and experienced the training of a Tonto Apache warrior.

Daily, Seesoff rode from her camp to the store and arrived at 8:00 a.m. Billy would be up, fed, and dressed by Dan. Seesoff played all morning with Billy using props from the store and she also taught him Indian games. Then came snack time. They continued with lessons on Apache language and customs. It was Dan's belief that Billy should understand the Indian culture. The boy could then live in harmony with the Indians as he grew older. During naptime Seesoff cleaned and tidied the living quarters. After lunch they played some more, then stories about Apache legends and culture preceded another nap. While Billy napped, Seesoff assisted Dan in the store with many tasks. After preparing the evening meal Seesoff rode home. Dan and Billy spent the evening reading, writing, practicing math, discussing history and business, and studying the Bible. Dan arranged for Billy to spend time at Buckskin Hat's camp learning Apache ways. This included training for becoming an adult in the tribe and a warrior.

As time went by, Billy stopped doubling up with Seesoff on her horse and rode his own. Dan bought the horse, which was selected by Buckskin Hat from the Indian herd. Billy learned horsemanship from both army personnel and his Indian family. The major training objective for Apache boys was to gain proficiency in activities connected with raiding and warfare. One of the culminating activities was to carry out a mock raid, not actually stealing horses, but showing agility and skill. Billy and his Indian brothers approached a camp, usually another Indian camp, within a mile. From this vantage point they planned a raid. The older men then commented on the plan. They discussed actual raids and warfare from the past. This was a valuable lesson for the trainees.

Although he was young for the training, Billy was allowed to participate because he was big for his age and had performed well on preliminary activities. He was included because of the insistence of Buckskin Hat. Although the raiding and warfare training was based on fighting soldiers and settlers, Buckskin Hat declared that Billy must be treated like any Indian boy in spite of his white skin. "Billy is my son, a member of my family," he said. "He is to be known as White Warrior with all the respect due him."

Billy's training ended abruptly when hostilities between the United States Army and the Indians increased. He had to stop visiting the camp. Seesoff was told by Buckskin Hat to stop her work at the store. She had become like a mother to Billy and the boy was twelve years old when she left. He lost a mother for a second time. On the last day of her work, Seesoff talked with Billy, bringing him readily into tears.

"Billy, keep your mind free to take any path in your life," she said. "Try to remember the many lessons we have learned together." She hugged him. "You are White, I am Indian— you must work hard to become a strong and good White man. With the war that is coming, you will hear bad things about the Indians. You know who we are; we are not what they say. Think kindly of your Indian family. I will be thinking of you and listening to the signs of how you are doing. War cannot last forever. When all this is over, find where the army has put us and come to see me. Buckskin Hat is preparing for war against General Crook. He wants you to stay away from the camp." Seesoff took a ribbon from around her neck. "Here is a medallion to wear. This has our family crest and the sign of an Apache warrior. My father says this will give you safe passage among the tribes. Do not test the strength of this medal until this war is over. I love you, son. I will pray to my gods for your care and protection, and you pray to your Christian God and obey his Commandments."

Seesoff said good-bye to Dan, went out and mounted her horse, and rode off into the evening mist. She was not to be seen for some time.

# Chapter 4: The Settlement

Billy arose in the late morning. Mom Murphy greeted him with a large plate of ham and eggs. His arm and shoulder felt stiff and a little sore.

After breakfast Mildred trimmed Billy's black hair. She kept it cut at collar length. In an earlier fall he had wounded his head at the crown. The tuft of hair had grown back gray. Mildred commented on it each time she trimmed his hair.

A firm, square jaw and a straight nose beneath a broad forehead enhanced Billy's looks. He carried a kindly expression and impressed people with his quiet manner and magnetic smile. His muscular 6' 1" and 185-pound frame was an exceptional build for a seventeen-year-old boy. People remembered him. Billy had earned a reputation for being responsible and dependable. He practiced with his guns several hours each week and was considered to be someone to steer clear of, someone who was proficient with his weapons.

Billy moved into the café for some coffee and a talk with Mom and Dad Murphy. They had completed the lunch cleanup and were ready to talk with Billy.

"Billy," Mildred commented, "Charlee Rae was in early this morning to see how you were. The Darrows stayed in town last night and left for the ranch this morning. Charlee seems to be attached to you. She's smart and wholesome, and sure to grow up to be a beauty."

"She's okay," Billy gestured as he roamed around the kitchen looking for a snack.

"You need to be careful with her feelings. She needs special consideration."

Dad Murphy joined them and sat down with a cup of coffee. He was hankering to talk. "Billy, what happened on this scout?"

Mildred and Duane sat attentively as Billy described the death of Jim Ream and the gun battle with the intruders. "I probably killed two or three men, and it isn't a good feeling." Mildred turned pale and choked back tears.

"You did what you had to, son!" Duane said. "We can't allow these marauders to come in and attack us. We have to respond. You did well."

His eyes glowed alive and triumphant as he gave Billy a firm handshake and a hug. Mildred sat sobbing and dabbing her eyes with a handkerchief. "I'm afraid for you, Billy," she said, trying to compose herself. "You need to be with more men when you do these things." Billy smiled and soothed her by giving assurances he would be careful. He knew there would be a need for a point scout, working out in front, alone.

It was a bright day as Billy left the Murphy place to check on his horse at the stable. George Blake operated the livery and a blacksmith shop. Freighters and coach companies would leave changeover stock at Blake's stables. There were corrals in back for horses and cattle.

Billy stopped in to see George and inquired after his family. The Blakes' living quarters were adjacent and upwind of the livery. They had three sons and a daughter. George Blake was a large man and normally put in a brutal workday.

"Hello, Billy," George offered as he saw the young man approach. "I heard about your work with those intruders. We need to find a way to protect ourselves from this kind of thing."

Billy agreed. "Some people say we should have a militia or standing posse."

George thought on the possibility as he tapped on a horseshoe. "There would have to be a system to warn people and call in the members. Gunshots would sound a couple of miles. There could be secondary shots to pass on the call. It would take two or three hours to get ten to fifteen riders in. We need to talk to Brady the next time he's here."

Billy was interested in what George had to say. A major concern was how to protect the settlement; it was a main attraction for renegades like Rudd Leland and area gangs as well as rogue Indians off the reservation.

Billy wandered down past the large water well in the middle of the street. It had served the settlement originally, but there were other wells developed as things grew. Buried pipes had been run from private wells to the buildings. The water from the runoff in the surrounding hills replenished the groundwater.

Cowboys from the surrounding area frequented the settlement. Ranchers supplied their spreads through the business services. Miners were supplied from Murphy's. Soldiers, freighters, merchants, and various coach passengers made the settlement a growing commerce center.

Billy stopped at Pike's saloon to say hello to Pike Graves, the owner. Pike's place was the social center for the rough crowd. Pike offered services common on the frontier. Drinks, cards, and conversations constituted the activities. There were also the saloon girls, Molly and Liz, who had seen the downside of life and were drifting in despair.

Billy's relationship with Pike was tolerant and charitable. Pike enjoyed Billy's talk about hunting and mining. Molly and Liz were happy to see him because he treated them with respect and consideration.

"Billy, I understand you had a little trouble with some intruders over at the breaks," Pike commented wryly. "Heard you got nicked by a bullet. Shows you're human like the rest of us."

Billy smiled and said, "I hope we won't have to fight them off at our doorstep. We're vulnerable here in the settlement, and there aren't enough guns to put up against a bunch like Rudd Leland's gang. We would have to hold until help came. How, I don't know." The place grew silent as Billy worked his way out the door.

The sky was beginning to cloud up as Billy continued down the street past the jail. The jail had two holding cells and small quarters for Ira Brady when he was in town. Prisoners were held until the jail wagon came by to pick them up. The wagon had a regular route, picking up prisoners and taking them to Verde for the circuit court. Convicted prisoners were sent to prison near Prescott. Duane Murphy had been appointed justice of the peace and had administrative functions, police power, and judicial authority over certain crimes.

At the end of the street was the social hall, where social and community meetings were held. The walls were thick and laced with gun ports. In case of an attack, the building could be defended.

Billy crossed the street to Dr. Pierce's office. As Billy entered he met Mrs. Jorgensen, who was in the family way. She gently squeezed his arm, "We're proud of you, Billy, for what you do to help protect us."

Billy smiled, said thank you, and moved past her as she was leaving.

Dr. Pierce greeted Billy. "Come on in, Hoss. Let's look at those wounds." He unwrapped the bandages and examined the wounds. "These look good. It's important to freshen the bandages regularly. You will have some rough scars on your forearm, but the shoulder should heal clean." Billy paid the doctor, greeted Mrs. Pierce, and moved up the street back to the Murphys' place.

Murphy had a general merchandise store, supplemented by a small café and rooming facility. Duane Murphy had bought the prefabricated building from the Lyman Bridges Company in Chicago. It was shipped in and built on the site. There was a large space in the store for visitors to sit and talk around a cracker barrel, gossiping and discussing concerns. Murphy's also served as an unofficial post office. Couriers and coaches would leave and pick up mail on their way through.

Duane Murphy was strong physically, mentally, and spiritually. He had been a cavalry officer in the war but then gave up his commission to move into business. A quiet man, Duane was the soul of the community, inseparable from the life and culture. When he spoke, it was like lightning in a dry summer sky—the ensuing thunder was the power of his message.

In the back, off the living quarters, Duane had placed a strong safe. He held important papers, gold, and currency for the community. Murphy had placed a metal cage around the safe. The cage was made by the blacksmith and anchored to the floor with bolts and cement blocks. The safe and the cage had separate locks.

Billy paused in his walk and stood still. He surveyed the layout of the settlement. This was a growing area; commerce was developing and people would stay. Stronger law and order was needed. The settlement looked forlorn, but the dreams of the people reflected hope for a better life.

Billy walked into Murphy's store. Customers milled about, shopping and socializing. When they saw him, they stopped and grew silent. Newcomers did not know Billy. He heard "scout" and "gunfighter." His eyes looked about and fell briefly to the floor. These labels were not what he wanted; he was much more than that in his own mind. To escape their stares, he walked quickly to the gun section to work on weapons dropped off for repair, but this only drew attention from the crowd; it seemed to fit his image.

# Chapter 5: Charlee Rae
# Talks to Dr. Pierce

The water from the stream, running the northern border of the ranch house clearing, was glimmering to gold by the rising sun. The Darrows ate their usual hefty breakfast. Billy's exploits from the scout had been the talk of the settlement for almost a week and still held the Darrows' conversation.

"Billy has to find something else to do with his life or he will be lost to us by drifting away or being killed," Bertha commented worriedly. She was becoming more concerned about the relationship between Billy and Charlee.

Charlee stiffened at the thought and blurted, "He needs more ideas put into his mind. I want him to think of me and what my plans are." Bertha had told Willard about Charlee's feelings for Billy. Willard jostled the table as he reached for another biscuit.

"Billy is doing more thinking about his future than you might believe," Willard offered. He seemed disturbed by the persistence of the topic of conversation. "Billy has been buying cattle and has a contract with me to run them with ours. We have chosen to keep it a little quiet so as not to start gossip."

"What gossip?" Charlee demanded.

Bertha chimed in, "Let's calm down and be careful what we are saying. Charlee, don't let this get out of hand."

"Dad, what are his plans?" Charlee insisted.

"I don't really know except for the cattle and our discussion on ranch land and such."

Charlee pushed back her chair and came to her feet. "Mom! Dad! You know how I feel. Why haven't you told me?"

Bertha, seeking to halt the line of conversation, said firmly, "Let's let Dad find out more from Billy as to what he is thinking, and then we can talk."

Willard and Charlee seemed to welcome this compromise, and they ate breakfast in silence for a bit.

Moments later Charlee blurted, "After Billy was here last week with his wounds, I feel it is important for us to know more about treating sick and injured people. I would like to talk to Dr. Pierce about staying in town a day or two each week and assisting him with his work. I would like to train as a medical assistant, maybe go to Prescott for a few weeks to work at the clinic and hospital."

This news stunned Bertha and Willard. Bertha was quick to respond, "You might be too young to go to Prescott. Maybe a day or two with Dr. Pierce might be acceptable. What do you think, Dad?" Willard mused at the thought of Charlee tending sick and injured people in town. He could just picture the attitude of people.

Charlee sensed his concern and muttered, "I don't care what people think—only you two and Billy."

Willard gave guarded approval by suggesting she talk to Dr. Pierce.

\*\*\*

A few days later Charlee was in town with Willard to pick up some grain. "May I go over and talk to Dr. Pierce, Dad?" Before he could answer, Charlee sprang into a fast walk toward Dr. Pierce's office.

Dr. Pierce warmly welcomed Charlee into his office. "What can I do for you, Charlee?" he said as he pointed her to a seat.

"I'm interested in becoming a doctor's assistant so I can help the community. I could assist you for a while, and then go to Prescott for a few weeks to train in the clinic and hospital."

Dr. Pierce sat up straight then nestled back into his stuffed chair. "I don't know if this is possible," he told her, "particularly the Prescott thing. I have friends over there. I'll inquire and get back to you." He sat up again. "You're kind of young to take this on. I don't know how people will look on it."

Charlee showed little concern. "People don't like the fact that I can ride, shoot, and run cattle as good as anybody. I won't let the attitude of others hold me back. I only care about what you and the people in Prescott think."

Dr. Pierce remarked, "I know you're sixteen going on twenty. This seems to be the impression most people have of you." Charlee was pleased with that appraisal. "Charlee, what do Bertha and Willard think of these ideas?"

Charlee quipped, "They are fine with it. They are a little concerned over staying all night in the settlement and going to Prescott. I need to assure them I'm mature enough to do this."

Charlee left Dr. Pierce's office and walked down the street

to see if Billy was home.

Mildred was working in the kitchen and was surprised to see Charlee. "Charlee Rae, how are you? I've been thinking about you." Charlee went in and posted herself next to the table. "Charlee, what is your interest in Billy?"

Charlee was quick to reply. "I love him and want to be his wife, live at Arrow, and have a family." The surge in Charlee's voice astonished Mildred.

"Do you believe you and Billy are ready for this?" Mildred challenged.

"Maybe not now, but soon."

"Have you discussed this with Billy?"

"I know he cares for me and wants me the same way I want him, but no, we haven't discussed these feelings." Mildred was irritated by the apparent presumptions of Charlee. She seized the moment to remind Charlee she should not make this claim without talking to Billy.

Charlee, not halted by Mildred's comments, replied, "What would you think of the idea, Mrs. Murphy?" Charlee's pressing the point caught Mildred off guard.

"I don't feel right discussing this until you talk to Billy." Mildred retreated into the hotel lobby to break the moment. Charlee sat for a spell then left the café.

In a few weeks Charlee was working with Dr. Pierce. She spent two days and one night each week in the settlement. She stayed with the Pierces, which gave her many opportunities to see Billy and to build relations with Duane and Mildred. She needed to convince the Murphys she was worthy of Billy's affections.

# Chapter 6: Showdown at Pike's

It was a cool, blustery day. Billy had just finished tuning some guns that had been left for conditioning. The Murphys sold new and used guns, an active business in the territory, and Duane had passed his gunsmith knowledge on to Billy.

Billy was helping Duane stock a recent shipment of merchandise when the door of Murphy's place burst open, aided by the wind and headed by one of the Blake children.

"Mr. Murphy," the boy cried, "three men have Clay Sprague cornered in the saloon. My dad is out at a ranch fixing a wheel. Mr. Graves sent me to get you and Billy."

"I'll check it, Dad," Billy said as he looked at the load in his Colt.

"I'll be along right away. Careful, you don't know who they are or what to expect." Duane moved toward the living quarters to get his gun.

Billy strode up the street and approached Pike's place at the front door. The swinging door was closed because of the wind. Billy peered through the window. He could see three men standing abreast, facing Clay Sprague. The men were at one end of the bar and Clay was in the middle, facing them.

Billy opened the door with his left hand, keeping his right near the butt of his Colt. As he stepped in, the men swung to face him. "What's the problem, Pike?" Billy said as he sized up the men.

"These guys have been hassling us. Clay came in and confronted them," Pike explained angrily.

Billy noticed Clay was not wearing a gun. The men were armed and wearing their guns as if they intended to use them. "What do you fellas want?" Billy asked.

Billy heard a whispered laugh. "We are just having a little fun," muttered a small man with a twitch in his cheek.

"What do they call fun, Pike?" Billy asked the barkeep.

"They haven't paid. They shoved tables and chairs around. Billy, they've mistreated the girls."

Disturbed, Billy turned to the girls. "Molly, Liz, you okay? Did they hurt you?"

"They twisted our arms and pushed us around," Liz complained.

Billy's hand was resting on his Colt. He confronted the man who seemed to be the leader. "We don't allow people to come here and harass our citizens. You men stand steady and don't let your gun hands drift. If you do, I'll shoot you."

The leader, a large, stocky man, looked at Billy and said, "You must be the shootist we heard about."

"Yes, I am. We're not going to allow you or anyone else to hurrah our settlement."

The third man stood quietly, holding a smoke.

The leader shifted his gun hand toward his belt. With a raking move Billy drew and cocked his Colt, and bared it directly at the man's chest. The man turned pale and lifted his hands. The others froze in place, petrified by Billy's swift action.

"You're close to being shot," Billy said grimly. "With your off hand, drop your gun belts to the floor. Push them behind you with a foot." He turned to Clay. "Pick them up." Billy noticed out of the corner of his eye, Duane standing with a shotgun ready.

"Is everything under control here, Billy?" Duane asked as he looked at the scene.

"You men, this is Duane Murphy, justice of the peace. We have to talk to him about what we're going to do about you. In the meantime, we're putting you in jail."

Billy and Clay marched the men down to the jail. Inside, Billy put two men in one cell and the leader in the other. Billy explained, "I will bring some water pitchers, basins, cups, and towels. There is a honey bucket in each cell." After some complaining, the men were forced to settle into their circumstances.

Billy and Clay met with Duane at the store to discuss actions to be taken.

"We can charge these men with several minor crimes. They need to be sent on their way by tomorrow," Duane reasoned.

Clay claimed, "They treated the women harshly and could be charged with assault."

Billy added, "The jail wagon won't be around for another week and Brady about the same time. We would have to hire someone to run the jail until that time."

"The settlement has no budget at this time," Duane complained. "I could find them guilty of assault and disturbing the peace. These charges could warrant us sending them to Verde. We could hold them tonight and send them on their way tomorrow. Or I could put them on probation. If they show up here again, we would jail and send them to Verde."

They concurred that Duane's idea would be a good solution. The three walked down to the jail and explained the decision to the men. After several repeated explanations by Duane, the men accepted the conditions.

The next day Billy and Duane got the men's gear and horses, and walked down to the jail. The gun rigs were stuffed in the saddlebags along with a light meal prepared by Mildred.

Opening the cell doors, Billy instructed the men to empty the honey buckets at the latrine in back, wash and return them to the cell. This caused some complaining from the men.

Billy mused, "You are getting off easy. We took five dollars from each of your pokes to pay for food, drinks, and glass damage in the saloon."

Billy escorted them out of the settlement and told them not to come back. The leader asked, "Shootist, would you have gunned me before I touched my gun?"

"Yes," Billy responded.

"I thought so," the man said with a wry smile.

Billy watched them out of sight as they headed south.

# Chapter 7: The Capture of Charlee Rae

Since Charlee Rae had been working with Dr. Pierce in town, Willard insisted she have a two-man escort to and from the settlement. The six-mile trip to town ran through flat land, rolling hills, and some canyons. Charlee was armed with her Colt and saddle gun, and could use them well.

A chill shivered through the October air. The weather was changing and Charlee felt it that morning. She and her escort were taking the early morning trek to the settlement. Charlee slid down from her horse and said, "I need to take a little rest here and go behind the bushes." She bustled off toward a stand of cottonwood laden with bushes and grass.

Charlee had finished her nature's call and was starting back to the others, when without warning she was wrenched to the ground, gagged, blindfolded, and hands bound. Her captors pushed her astride a horse and tied her feet underneath. She could hear Indians talk as the horse was led away. The lead was slow and quiet for a short distance, then the pace quickened. Her hands were tied with a rope around the horse's neck so she could hang on.

This flight went on for what seemed to be hours. Finally, they arrived at an encampment and people began jostling her horse and making noise. She was wrestled from the horse and placed in a wickiup. What felt like an eternity went by before two Indians entered, untied her, and took off the blindfold.

"What are you doing? What do you want?" Charlee asked. Only silence. One Indian was older and seemed to be in charge. The younger Indian left and came back with water and bread. She reluctantly took the food and drank and ate as she watched the two look her up and down. The men finally left, and she noticed a guard was placed outside the door. Charlee was a captive, where and for what reason she didn't know.

The two escort riders waited a reasonable time before calling out to Charlee, "Come on, Charlee, we need to go." Hearing no response they rode over to the trees and found her gone. They found tracks of four or five unshod horses and followed for a hundred yards or so. The signs told it clearly. One rider shouted, "You go to tell the Darrows. Leave her horse here. I'll ride to town to get Billy."

Billy was preparing to go out to a ranch to track and kill a rogue bear for a friend. The escort rider rode directly to Murphy's place, found Billy, and told him about Charlee's capture. Pale with the news, Billy instructed the rider to wait. He asked Mildred to pack some jerky and biscuits. He was already dressed for a scout. The Sharps had to be exchanged with the Winchester '73. Billy checked for water, shells, an extra Colt, and bandages. These were placed in his pommel bag, which Mildred had stuffed with food. He grabbed his outfit and briskly walked to his horse. Mildred followed in a fright. "Billy," she said, "You be careful. Don't lose your caution because it's Charlee. I know how you feel about her."

"I know, Mom. I will bring her back and kill anyone who has harmed her." This stern manner was not characteristic of Billy, and Mildred wrung her hands, concerned about his judgment yet aware he had no choice but to go.

Billy and the rider galloped out of town toward the place where Charlee had been captured. Riders from Arrow arrived to find Billy reading the signs. "Six unshod horses, leading at a walk first, then into a slow trot." A shaken Willard Darrow ran up.

"What is it, Billy?" Willard whispered.

"They have Charlee and are heading to the hills on the west. There is a band of Tontos camped about three miles in. She may be there. We can't charge in and risk something happening to her in a firefight." He looked Willard square in the eye. "The Apache tribe adopted me as a boy. I have a warrior's medallion around my neck." Billy pulled the medal out of his shirt to show Willard, "I will try to use it to get into the camp, find out if she is there, and get her out. You fellas follow along slowly for about a mile and wait for me there. If I'm not back by nightfall, send for help and hold them until you find out what has happened."

"Maybe we should follow you closer and be ready to strike if something goes wrong?" Willard said, shaking his head.

"No." Billy looked directly at the older man. "We don't have time to discuss this any more. If the Apaches feel we are a threat to them, they may put a bullet in her head and retreat further into the hills. We don't know why they took her or what plans they have. Maybe we can buy her back without anybody getting killed."

Willard reluctantly agreed. Billy moved out with his horse

at a trot. Shadows were gathering and growing longer down the canyons. Time was working against Billy and he spurred his horse faster. The trail was easy to follow. He planned to move fast for a ways and then slow down to read signs more carefully.

As he walked his horse along, Billy noticed one rider had dropped off to the side of the trail and climbed up a grassy slope to the right. Billy retreated to get a clear look at the land ahead. He reasoned that the bunch had left a man behind as a lookout for pursuers. Billy had to go around behind the slope to find the lookout before he was seen.

Tying off his horse, Billy slipped his Winchester from the scabbard. To the right of the grassy knoll he located where the Apache had come up from the trail and ridden into some trees. Billy knelt to a crawl, working his way around and above the trees. He spotted the man's tethered horse and studied the trees until he located the lookout. The Indian was sitting comfortably against a tree watching the back trail. Billy slipped in behind the man and surprised him by a clout with the butt of his Winchester. The Apache rolled over on his side, sat up, and rose to his feet. He was confronted by Billy standing with the Winchester leveled at the Indian.

"I am a warrior of the Apache tribe. I am the adopted son of Buckskin Hat, the great Apache chief. You have taken a captive into your camp. I have come to claim her. She is my woman." Billy knew ownership of Charlee would lend him negotiating power.

Billy showed his medallion and said, "You go to the camp and tell your shaman or chief what I have said, and I will follow later." Confused, the Indian retreated to his horse and rode off toward the camp. Billy ran to his horse and rode hard up the trail. He wanted to find the camp to observe it and to see if they would send out riders to meet him.

Billy found the camp and used his glass to study the activity. The gathered warriors talked excitedly. Two riders were sent up the trail and posted themselves. The women and children in the camp were sent inside the wickiups. The men spread out around the camp, rifles in hand. Billy counted twenty-five well-armed warriors. He wondered if he was riding into a death trap but knew he had no choice.

Billy rode into the camp slowly, escorted by the two warriors who had been posted on the trail. He held his medallion up above his head and kept his other hand away from his guns. He stopped in front of the apparent leader and slid off his horse. "I am White Warrior from the family of Buckskin Hat. I am an Apache warrior."

"I am Claw Hand, chief of this camp. I remember you from years past. You used to come to our camps to learn our ways. Why are you here?"

Billy walked within six feet of Claw Hand. He pressed his right hand, palm in, against his chest. This gesture showed he held no weapon and placed over the heart reflected sincerity.

Billy took a breath, collected himself, and said, "Some of your men have taken my woman and brought her here. If she has been harmed, someone will answer to me. I wish to see her now."

Claw Hand stood expressionless but was pleased with the bravery of this warrior. "One of my subchiefs has seen this woman on the trail and stalked her until she was captured. He did not know she was the woman of another warrior."

Sensing Claw Hand's position, Billy said, "I know you, as chief, own captives taken by your warriors. I am willing to give you two horses for your gift to me." He hoped this gesture would take the edge off the tension of the moment.

Claw Hand mused over the issue and moved over to a group of warriors. One warrior became angry and walked toward Billy. Claw Hand stopped the man and they argued in low voices.

Returning to Billy, Claw Hand said, "This subchief has claimed this woman for a wife and refuses to let you have her."

"I know you own her and can give her to me. He has no right of capture because she already belongs to me. I have made an offer of two horses in good faith. You may give them to him if you wish."

Claw Hand pondered his problem and walked over to the complaining warrior to present Billy's offer. After a heated discussion, Claw Hand returned.

"My warrior has claimed a right of combat to settle this problem. There is no clear right of combat in this case—you are not an outsider, you are an Apache. I must think on this and decide."

"I want to be taken to my woman while you are deciding." Claw Hand escorted Billy to the guarded wickiup. Billy entered through the thatched door and was embraced by Charlee. "Billy, I'm so scared. I thought they were going to kill me." Billy explained the circumstances and that the warrior wanted her for a wife.

"A wife! If he comes at me I'll wreck him."

"Say nothing, be obedient, and walk behind me with your head down. This will be expected of an obedient Apache wife."

"You told them I was your wife?" She blushed and smiled warmly.

"It seemed a way to help get you out," Billy quipped. In a serious tone he added, "If he won't give in, I will have to kill him in combat, or he me." Billy knew he would have to get something done soon or Willard and the posse would charge in and a lot of people would be killed.

Claw Hand returned to the wickiup and said, "The warrior will accept three horses for the interest in this woman."

"You have an agreement." Billy was greatly relieved by the decision.

"You will sit with my council to discuss these terms."

As Billy left the wickiup he told Charlee to stay calm and that he would be back to get her.

"I am afraid, Billy," she said, holding his arm.

"So am I. I might have to fight that warrior if something goes wrong."

Billy left Charlee and went to the council to sit with them and talk. Claw Hand said, "Our scouts tell us there is a group of riders about three miles down the trail. What are they going to do? What is your word?"

"The woman is the daughter of a chief among the White people. They are there to help her if needed. I asked them to stay until I return. I will get the three horses from them and return. By nightfall this incident will be over."

"Good," Claw Hand said as he rose to his feet.

The meeting was over and Claw Hand escorted Billy to the wickiup. Billy asked, "Claw Hand, could you give her a Tonto name and a ceremonial belt indicating she is an Apache of some regard. I wish to give her some protection in the future."

Claw Hand said he would think about it.

Billy told Charlee he was going to get the horses and come back for her. She pleaded with him to hurry.

Billy rode hard down the trail toward the posse. The shadows in the canyons were deep and night was not far off.

He came upon the men by surprise. "What would happen if I were leading a band of Tontos? You have no guards out." This was the scout in him. He gave the men a brief explanation as to what had happened. "Throw the saddles off three horses and give me Charlee's," Billy directed. "Tie them for me to a lead."

He went to his pommel bag to get some jerky and biscuits. He had not eaten all day. If for some reason the warrior changed his mind and Billy had to fight him, he would need all his strength.

Up from the posse came the comment, "This story is kind of wild. I think we ought to ride in there; there are twenty of us. We could take Charlee and teach those Indians a lesson."

"Who said that?" Billy shouted.

Clay Sprague rose and said defiantly, "I did."

"Clay," Billy replied, "they are ready for us. There are twenty-five well-armed warriors to meet us. These are not the garden keepers we see in the valley, these are great warriors who fought General Crook viciously up through '73. There are still bands of Apaches all over this territory that have refused to go to the reservation at Fort Verde. These warriors are under Chief Claw Hand and will fight if pushed too hard."

Darrow stepped forward. "She is my daughter and I want to follow Billy's plan."

Billy took the horses in tow and led them toward the Indian camp. About one mile from the camp two warriors met him and escorted him in. Claw Hand handed the horses to the offended warrior. He took them and reluctantly walked away, disturbed.

Relieved, Billy dropped from his horse and walked toward the wickiup where Charlee was kept. She was cleaned up and strikingly beautiful. Charlee went to Billy, gave him a hug, and kissed him on the cheek. "Thank you, Billy," she said as they prepared to leave.

Billy reminded her, "Apache women are obedient; follow behind me and don't say a word."

"That will be the day! Obedience stuff…," Charlee grumbled. Billy smiled as they left the wickiup.

They walked toward Claw Hand, Charlee following. Billy gave the peace sign, open palm to the chest. He handed his bowie knife to Claw Hand, saying, "This is a special gift to a great chief and warrior."

The couple walked toward their horses. Suddenly from behind a wickiup a figure darted out and struck Billy in the back with a war club. Billy dropped to his knees from the blow and instinctively spun to face his enemy. There was the disgruntled warrior shouting, "I claim right of combat!" The warrior rushed Billy. From his kneeling position, Billy met the charge by coming up underneath the man with an arm-bar, hip-lock throw, putting the warrior on his back. Holding the man's left arm Billy rotated and dislocated his opponent's shoulder, and placed his foot on the other man's neck. Looking at Claw Hand, he declared, "Do you want him dead or will Apache law deal with him?"

Claw Hand was stunned by the incident. "He has shamed us. We will deal with him under our law of safe passage."

The man lay writhing in pain from the dislocated shoulder. Charlee stepped forward and told Billy, "Have some men hold him; I will set the shoulder."

Billy told Claw Hand that Charlee was a medicine woman and could help the man. Three warriors grabbed the man to hold him still. Charlee sat down, placing one foot on the neck of the man, the other under the armpit of the injured shoulder. She rotated the arm firmly and the shoulder slipped back in place. She rose and asked Billy to get the bag off her horse. She took out a small bottle of laudanum and gave it to Claw Hand. "Billy, tell him to give half of this tonight and the rest tomorrow. This will help the pain. He needs to keep the man's arm still for a few days until the pain is gone."

Billy turned to Claw Hand and gave him Charlee's instructions. The people in the camp were awed by what they had just seen.

Claw Hand stepped forward, "From this time on, this person is an Apache woman. I give her the name White Fawn. I take her as a daughter in my family." He handed her a ceremonial belt, placed his hand on her shoulder, and said, "May the spirit bless you and White Warrior with many sons." Charlee smiled and bowed. She nudged Billy as they walked to their horses.

They rode slowly out of the camp, picking up the pace as they moved out of sight. After a short ride they came upon two lookouts from the posse and rode on to meet the others.

Charlee flew from her horse to embrace her father. Everyone was relieved. Even Clay Sprague mumbled, "I still don't believe all this story." The group returned to the road. Some went into the settlement and others to Arrow. Willard asked Billy to come to the ranch so he could get the full story of the incident. Billy asked the men going into the settlement to tell the Murphys what had happened and that he would be home late in the evening or the next morning.

Approaching the ranch they were met by a shriek from Bertha as she ran to embrace Charlee. She reached and rested her hand on Billy's leg as he sat his horse. "Thank you, Billy, for your skill and daring to do this for us."

"I did it for me as much as for anybody, because it was

Charlee." Bertha knew Billy would be the key person in such a safe recovery. Billy smiled and rode toward the house. He slid from his horse, wincing from the pain in his back caused by the blow from the war club. He walked down to the washbasin at the water tank. Dog-tired, with muscles sodden and fatigued, Billy struggled to get his shirt off.

Willard joined alongside and started to wash. "Hoss, that's a nasty bruise on your back. Someone needs to look at it." Willard splashed his face. "This country is so hard and dangerous, Billy. I need to talk to you about your plans and about Charlee. It can wait though—let's get something to eat."

They drifted casually into the house. Billy and Willard sat down and served themselves some coffee. Bertha joined them as she waited for stew to season on the stove. Charlee had cried with her mother for a time and they had retreated to her room for a hot bath. Bertha said, "Charlee has bruises and scrapes. What about this, her being your wife?"

Billy, a little flustered, replied, "I had to think of something to take the ownership of her away from that Tonto warrior. He had been stalking her along the trail for some time, waiting for a chance to take her. He had a love for her and was ready to fight to the death for her."

"So were you," Bertha said looking into Billy's eyes. "Do you love Charlee Rae, Billy?"

The fatigue of the ordeal dulled Billy. He was slow to comprehend what Bertha was asking. "I do as far as I can at this time. She is young and so am I. She is lovely, strong, and talented—more than I could hope for." Charlee entered the room, clean and brushed in a fresh cotton print dress. There was an abrupt hush to the conversation with her sudden presence.

At the table, Charlee exuberantly talked of Billy's exploits

51

with the Apaches. She told of the hardships but felt she came out of the experience a stronger person. "After all, I am a Tonto woman named White Fawn. I have a ceremonial belt to protect me. Best of all, I am married to the courageous Apache White Warrior." An aura of suspense hung over the room but Charlee did not notice. Bertha mulled over Billy's earlier words as she watched her daughter gaze at the young man.

Billy rose from the table. Finishing his coffee and munching on a sweet roll, he told Willard he would like a fresh horse. "I need to get home to see Dad and Mom Murphy. They will be worried."

Charlee protested, though Bertha agreed Billy should go home.

"This has been quite a day," Willard sighed as they eased out of the kitchen and onto the porch. A ranch hand brought Billy a fresh horse and moved his saddle and gear to the new mount. Billy checked everything to see if things were in order. He gave particular attention to his spare Colt in the pommel bag.

The extra attention to his outfit was partly to deflect the attention he was getting from Charlee. She had followed them out and was edging closer to Billy. Bertha watched with a frown. Billy started to mount, but Charlee held his arm, turned and embraced him long and hard. "Thank you for saving me." Softly she murmured, "I love you."

Billy smiled as he stepped smoothly into his saddle and turned toward the settlement. "I'll be seeing you soon folks. Good-bye, White Fawn." With a little laugh he reined his horse to a walk and then a slow trot.

The Darrows stood motionless as they watched Billy ride off in the dimming of the daylight. Willard said, "We have seen today, in all that's happened, the courage and spirit needed to tame this country. Billy, the Tontos, and all of us have learned from this."

Falling readily into tears, Bertha cried, "My family will never be the same."

Charlee gazed at the trail where Billy had gone.

# Chapter 8: Charlee Rae, Medicine Woman

At seventeen, Charlee had completed almost two years of training with Dr. Pierce. She knew she would have to work for acceptance as a medicine woman, but there was a need for medical care on the frontier and Charlee aimed to fill it.

A variety of experiences shaped her training. In addition to treating people in town, she often visited Indian camps in the area. These Indians had drifted off the reservations and lived peacefully in the hills. Billy went along as an escort. It was helpful to have an Apache warrior along. She also had her Apache name from Claw Hand, White Fawn.

Billy knew the medicine man at one of the camps. One day, he and Charlee rode into the camp, which lay in a small valley. An ample stream ran through the camp and there were patches of grass for grazing. Billy had given the residents a few head of cattle to help them through hard times.

Two warriors intercepted the couple and escorted them into the camp. Billy introduced Charlee as White Fawn from the Claw Hand family. He claimed her as his wife to discourage any amorous interest in her.

As they rode into camp, Billy placed his open hand against his chest as the peace sign. Charlee did the same. The chief, Cloud Maker, met them. After exchanging pleasantries, as friends expect, Billy asked, "Can we speak to your shaman? White Fawn is a medicine woman with the Whites. She wishes to learn from your shaman."

"She is welcome," Cloud Maker responded. "We will ask the shaman if he wishes to talk to her."

Billy and Charlee stepped off their horses and followed the chief up a small knoll on the left, beyond the stream. The Indian medicine men used an abundance of water in their medical treatments.

A small wickiup nestled against the backside of the knoll. This was the medicine house and home of the shaman. On the right side of the medicine house stood a sweat lodge made of willow branches and covered with animal skins. In the middle of the lodge lay a circular pile of rocks. Rocks, heated in fires and then sprinkled with water, produced steam. The steam could be healing.

The shaman was a small man with close-set eyes and a jagged scar across his left cheek. This made for a foreboding appearance. He carried an air of importance. The shaman was second only to the chief in the power of the tribe.

The chief stepped forward and talked briefly with the shaman. Then the chief moved aside and told Billy the shaman would speak with them. Billy spoke firmly. "I'm White Warrior, adopted son of Chief Buckskin Hat, and an Apache warrior. This is White Fawn, adopted daughter of Chief Claw Hand. She is my wife and a powerful medicine woman of the Whites."

The shaman took a strong step forward, directly confronting

Charlee. "You come to mock me and question my power."

Charlee stood firm, set her jaw and, as Billy interpreted, said, "I stand humbly before you. I wish to learn so I may help people. I wish to share some of my experiences," she paused, "if you wish. I am a child compared to your power."

The shaman, impressed with the humility and directness of this golden-haired woman, responded, "I have talked to White healers before and they were bigheaded and would not listen."

"I will listen and write down notes to record your wisdom." Charlee retrieved her notepad from her pack and showed it to the shaman.

Billy felt proud as he listened to Charlee converse with this powerful man. It was a comfortable day and they sat on some logs clustered to the side of the wickiup.

"I will tell you this as we start." The shaman shifted his leg as if it were stiff. He had what appeared to be a poultice on his neck. "Our religion is not separated from our medicine as with the Whites. You must understand and accept this. The ancient ones pass on much wisdom through the spirits we pray to."

With deep respect in her voice, Charlee said, "I believe in asking my God to help me in my life and work."

Pleased, the shaman said, "You speak well, medicine woman. Do not fail your god and he will send spirits to guide you."

Charlee and the shaman talked, comparing ideas on many treatments, until the sun settled low in the sky. At last, Billy noticed the shaman becoming restless. The sun was setting. He and Charlee had a five-mile ride back to the main road. The shaman agreed to conclude and preparations were made to leave.

As they stood by their horses, Charlee turned once more to the shaman and inquired about the poultice on the medicine man's neck. The shaman, surprised and reluctant, indicated it was an abscess he had been treating for some time. Charlee asked, "May I look at it and see if I can help?" Charlee's confidence was being tested and Billy struggled to make sure his interpretation was not condescending. The shaman nodded his approval.

Charlee removed the poultice and found an angry-looking boil, festered around the edges with a large pus core. She said, "Great one, I have learned to treat this sore by lancing the skin, squeezing the pus, and removing the core. This will make it heal faster and lessen the pain. Can I help you with this?"

The shaman looked Charlee in the eye, gave her a little smile, and told her, "I would appreciate your help." The sore had not responded to the poultice.

"Billy, would you get my bag from the horse and ask someone to bring hot water?"

Billy hesitated. "Are you sure you want to do this, Charlee?" Charlee nodded and smiled. Billy shook his head and also smiled. "I'll tell the chief what we are doing so he won't be alarmed." He walked to the chief's wickiup.

Charlee washed the area around the boil with water the shaman's granddaughter brought her, and dabbed the boil dry with clean rags. She swabbed the area with antiseptic and a local anesthetic. She took her scalpel and lanced the sore. With her tweezers she lifted the pus core out. She cleaned the wound and filled the cavity with an antiseptic salve to allow the wound to heal from the inside. She finished with a bandage.

"You will need to keep this bandage on for three days. I

will leave some of the salve to use when the bandage is changed. Repeat this until the wound is healed. It should heal in about two weeks."

Charlee cleaned up the work area and put the used rags in the fire. She praised the shaman. "You are a great man, and I am honored to have met with you. I would like to return someday and talk about some medical cases. If you need me to help, send word to White Warrior at the settlement."

"It was a good meeting," the shaman agreed. "It will be interesting to see how you grow in your work." The shaman turned to Billy. "She will give you strong sons." Then he turned and went into his home to rest.

Billy and Charlee made a hasty retreat from the camp. The shadows were dark in the washes. Early stars appeared in the dusky sky. They prodded their horses into a trot. Charlee had told her parents she would stay overnight at the Pierces.

They reached the main road and turned toward the settlement. A night haze gathered in the draws and entered the valley. Billy checked his Colt and the Winchester. Charlee did the same. This was good practice in a violent land. They rode abreast down the road and made small talk along the way.

"Billy, when are we going to have the sons the shaman mentioned?" Charlee smiled.

Recovering from his startled state, Billy replied, "Charlee, you will be going to Prescott soon for your training. I need to bring some things together to plan a future. I need to talk to your parents."

Charlee asked, "Don't you think I should be involved in some of this planning?"

"When the time comes," Billy said.

"Are you asking me to marry you, Billy?"

Billy pulled up his horse and faced Charlee. "I'm not in a position to do that right now."

Frustrated, Charlee mused. "Billy, you haven't told me you love me. Do you?"

Billy muttered shyly, "Yes, I do, but we must be careful about our relationship. Your mother is reluctant; your dad is cautious. We are young. They are afraid I'll be killed in the violence of this country. I have to change my ways and try to avoid some of these combat roles. This will be difficult for me and for the settlers. The settlement needs law and order, and defense capability. Like it or not, I feel some obligation to this defense."

Charlee lifted her leg over the saddle horn, leaned across, and kissed Billy long and hard. He caressed her gently and kissed her back. "I understand, Billy." Charlee shifted back into her saddle, spurred her horse, and the two rode off toward the settlement.

# Chapter 9: Charlee Goes to Prescott

Dr. Pierce arranged for Charlee to spend three months at the hospital and clinic in Prescott. She would volunteer to acquire the skills that would help her practice medicine in the settlement.

It was spring of 1878. Charlee was older and had matured through her experience at the clinic. She was physically and emotionally stronger and people had come to trust and respect her. She and Billy had an understanding about their relationship. It was no longer if they would be married, but when. Despite their commitment, her mother was still not completely supportive of her relationship with Billy. Charlee was hopeful that over time her mother would come to fully accept her relationship with Billy.

Charlee left the settlement on a commercial coach. A driver and guard manned the coach, and Willard Darrow and two of his cowboys rode along on horseback to add to the escort. They went to Verde and Charlee transferred to a coach escorted by soldiers. This was the regular stage running between Verde and Prescott. Darrow and the men would return home.

Before the stage left, Charlee spoke to Willard. "Dad, I want you to talk to Billy about his plans. He and I have agreed we are going to be married. He wants to get permission from you and Mom, but she doesn't like the idea of us being together. I don't want this to become a problem." She looked at her father. "Dad, I expect you to help me in this."

Willard moved his horse closer to the coach so he could talk more quietly. "We need to persuade your mother, not just tell her. You need to explain to her clearly how you feel. Write to her regularly. In the letters, persuade her you know what you're doing. I will talk to Billy about his plans. He will have to make some changes in his life to help ease your mother's mind."

The coach jolted as the driver climbed aboard. Charlee hurriedly asked, "Dad, how do you feel? Can I depend on your support?"

"Billy is stalwart, more than I could ask for in a son-in-law. I would be pleased to have him in our family, but I am worried about his safety and your welfare." The stage lurched forward under the charge of the horses, leaving the conversation drifting in their minds.

Prescott was an emerging mercantile center. As the coach approached the town Charlee noticed the beautiful mountain background and a pleasant scent of pines. Prescott was a booming mining town with a dominant whiskey row and its pleasure houses. The town shuddered under such rapid growth and its intrusion into the pristine area.

The stage arrived at the station at three o'clock in the afternoon. Charlee asked the station attendants how she could get to her boarding house by the hospital. The pretty young woman drew attention from men eager to help her with her luggage. Some of the offers irritated her and she became worried about getting to her rooming house. She felt relieved when a young army officer stepped forward. "Pardon me, may I be of service?" he asked with a bow. "I am Lieutenant Mark Evans."

"Thank you, sir," Charlee responded. "I need to get to my rooming house next to the hospital." A warm feeling came over her as she noticed the officer's courtesy.

The lieutenant motioned up the street. "It's within walking distance but your luggage will need to be transported by a carrier. Please wait and I'll go find someone to help."

Mark left and returned shortly with a man who would take the luggage to the rooming house. He gave the man instructions, paid him, and turned to Charlee. "May I have your name so this man can check your luggage at the rooming house?"

"My name is Charlee Rae Darrow."

"That's a nice name," Mark said. He was clearly taken by this lovely creature who had suddenly dropped into his life. "I would be pleased to escort you to your lodging," Mark said as he held out his arm. The politeness of the handsome soldier impressed Charlee and she slipped her arm through his. The warm feeling flushed again.

They walked casually down the boarded sidewalk. Mark was a West Point graduate and was with the cavalry stationed near Prescott. He hailed from New York. His stories of the big city reminded Charlee of a children's toy her mother cherished from her childhood, a kaleidoscope that made beautiful pictures, constantly changing.

At the boarding house—a neatly kept brown structure— Charlee's luggage sat on the porch beside woven chairs and a swinging bench. Mark walked up two stairs, approached and knocked on the door. A portly lady appeared. "I am Mrs. Gray. What can I do for you?"

Charlee stepped forward and introduced herself. "I am Charlee Rae Darrow. I have reservations to stay here for three months."

"Oh, yes," Mrs. Gray said, "I have been expecting you." As they walked to go into the house, Mrs. Gray stopped and addressed Mark. "Men callers," she said clearly, "must remain on the porch."

Mark replied, "I understand, ma'am." He faced Charlee and bowed. "Charlee, I beg your leave and will call on you again."

"Thank you," Charlee said with a nod. She followed Mrs. Gray into the house.

"You're a little flushed, dearie," Mrs. Gray said, looking Charlee up and down. "Remember, all men callers stay on the porch." Thus ended the first of many daily visits from Mark. He and Charlee sat on the porch swing and talked about their homes and lives. She was happy to have a friend to talk to and felt comfortable with Mark's presence.

The morning after she moved into the rooming house, Charlee went to the hospital. The hospital was a cottage with an outpatient clinic staffed by two doctors and three aides. The small building housed a waiting room, staff offices, an operatory, and a fifteen-bed ward. Dr. Sheffield, the doctor in charge of the hospital, met Charlee with a gruff admonition. "I expected you yesterday. You're out of uniform. Get two from the storeroom. The other ladies will show you." He moved off, other matters on his mind.

"Come on with me," one of the aides said with a smile on her face. "Don't let Dr. Sheffield bother you. He's gruff and nosy, but you will learn from him. Dr. Brown is another matter. He is quiet in manner and leaves you with worries about patients, things to correct, and clean up."

They went to the storeroom to get Charlee's uniforms. The uniform consisted of a long blue dress with long sleeves, a high neck, and a collar. A white pinafore apron was worn over the dress. A starched cap held the women's hair.

Charlee was treated as a probationary nurse. The doctors and aides called her a "probie." She cleaned and scrubbed floors and walls of an area before and after each admission. The patients were mostly bedridden. Charlee gave daily baths and changed sheets. She gave back massages to prevent bedsores. Bedpans were a regular chore.

Gradually Charlee worked into the treatment of patients. She applied carbolic acid solutions and dressings to infected wounds. She injected carbolic acid solutions into pus-filled cavities. She replaced surgical drains and tubes. She was expected to follow the doctor on his rounds to keep notes and record comments. Along the way she learned procedures and gained skills.

At the end of a twelve-hour day, Charlee returned to her room, ate a meal, and made sure her uniform was immaculate, ready for the next day.

Mark came by regularly to see her. They would sit and talk on the front porch swing. These were interesting discussions for Charlee. She learned about a kind of life and experiences completely different from her own. These discussions usually ended with her nodding off from exhaustion; before he excused himself, Mark would always take a few minutes to watch Charlee sleep. Once he moved a strand of hair from her cheek.

The days passed quickly between work and visiting. Two

weeks had passed and Charlee impressed the doctors with the knowledge she had acquired at the settlement with Dr. Pierce. Dr. Sheffield was taking time to meet with her to discuss her experiences at the Indian camps and frontier medicine in general. He recognized Charlee's gifts as a healer and began inviting her into surgery to observe and, later, to assist. The days were packed with enriching experiences for Charlee. She was becoming a genuine medicine woman.

On a warm, pleasant evening, Charlee and Mark were having their usual visit. Mark sat close to Charlee, smelling her fragrance and savoring her beauty. Soon, it was time for Charlee to go in. As they said good-bye at the door Mark whispered, "Charlee, I'm falling in love with you." He stepped closer and embraced her, kissing her gently but firmly on the lips.

Startled, Charlee drew back and stammered, "Good night, Mark."

Mark said good night and hastily walked off down the street. Charlee was shocked. What was that? she asked herself. What did I do to cause him to say those things and kiss me? I don't want a romance with him. I love Billy. Did I betray Billy? Poor Mark. Poor Billy. Charlee sat down again and then stood up. She went to her room, deep in thought.

Meanwhile, Billy had traveled to Verde to meet with a freighter to discuss buying wagons. He planned to lease them to a large freighting company that ran between Flagstaff, Prescott, Verde, and Globe. The wagons could be made in Verde or Prescott. This business trip was part of Billy's attempt to pull things together in preparation for his marriage to Charlee.

He decided to go on to Prescott to see Charlee. She had

been gone for about three weeks and Billy was lovesick thinking of her. Billy arrived in Prescott in the evening. He knew the town and took a shortcut through some pines to the rooming house. Charlee had described the rooming house in a letter written in her even hand.

Billy approached the house from the side, reined his horse, stepped off, and walked to the front. As he rounded the corner he saw Charlee and a soldier embracing. He saw the soldier kiss her. His heart sank. Anger swelled. He wanted to rush up and hurt the soldier but contained himself. Scouting had taught him to stay in control.

Billy remained in the shadows at the corner of the house. The soldier abruptly left and Charlee went into the house. Billy stood for a moment weighing what he had just seen. Charlee had evidently attracted the attentions of another man. It had never occurred to Billy that this would be a possibility. He walked back to his horse, mounted, and started toward home a disillusioned young man.

Charlee had written her mother and told her about meeting Mark and how interesting he was. Bertha had written back, encouraging her to give the relationship a chance to unfold. Charlee sat and visited with Mark two more times but her heart quivered as they talked. Charlee stopped seeing Mark altogether. She had work to keep her busy and she was eager to learn. She did not want any complications.

Charlee fretted over the lack of letters from Billy in recent weeks and was concerned he might go on another scout.

Her mother's letters shed no light. When she could stand it no longer, Charlee sat at her desk by the window and wrote Mildred Murphy to ask why Billy had not written. She waited for a reply.

***

When Billy returned home from his trip to Prescott, he told the Murphys about Charlee and the soldier. The incident had hurt Billy and had changed his thinking and planning. Mildred was worried. The Murphys knew their son as a strong and positive person. Now he seemed weakened by what he perceived as betrayal.

Billy moved on to two major issues in his life and tried to forget Charlee. He had received a letter from Buckskin Hat, who, in 1875, had been moved to the San Carlos Reservation from Verde. He was concerned about the welfare and safety of his family. He asked Billy if he would come and relocate Seesoff and Star, Billy's Indian sister, to the safer Tonto camps near Green Valley. These Indians had drifted back to the area and settled on land not used by the Whites. They lived off the land and did some work for the Whites, but the move would not be sanctioned by the army and they would have to do it secretly. Billy wanted to help move the women soon.

Billy also rededicated his effort to pursue and kill Rudd Leland. The army was mounting a campaign against Leland and had asked Billy to scout for them. Leland was responsible for the death of Billy's father. When Billy was twelve years old, he had vowed to avenge the death. He recalled the vow daily.

Duane and Mildred tried to persuade Billy he was not emotionally ready to do these things now, because of the incident with Charlee. Concerned for her son, Mildred replied to Charlee with a five-page letter and told her what Billy had seen and what was happening. She addressed the envelope and then, at the last minute, Mildred took the letter to Bertha

Darrow to share with her. She felt it was important for Bertha to know what was happening. The letter did not explain about the Indians or Rudd Leland. Mildred was concerned only that Charlee know about Billy seeing Charlee and the soldier, and that he was heartbroken.

"Please just send the letter along with your next one," Mildred asked Bertha when she saw her at the store. Bertha nodded and tucked the letter into her purse. Later, however, Bertha thought otherwise. She did not send the letter to Charlee, hoping her daughter's relationship with the soldier would warm into love. Bertha wanted Charlee freed from the fate of marrying a frontier scout and gunfighter.

# Chapter 10: Billy Relocates
## Seesoff and Star

Billy would travel about eighty miles on his trip to the San Carlos Reservation. He took two horses on a lead. Provisions for the trip were meager but this was necessary to prevent weighting the horses too heavily. They would have to travel fast at times to avoid army patrols. They would travel at night, conditions permitting.

Billy traveled at a good pace and was soon on the main road entering the reservation. He was easy on the horses to keep them in good shape for the trip back.

He had to avoid contact with John Clum, the Indian agent at San Carlos, and Al Sieber, chief scout for the army. They were acquaintances and Billy didn't want to compromise the relationship by helping two Apaches leave the reservation. He had met them through his scouting for the army and his mining trips into Apache country. Clum and Sieber were at San Carlos dealing with Geronimo and the unrest on the reservation.

There was a problem securing the two horses while he was

finding Buckskin Hat's camp. Billy led the horses into the livery behind the agency store. The proprietor was happy to earn a few extra dollars. Billy asked the store clerk if he knew where Buckskin Hat's camp was. The man knew where the camp was because Buckskin Hat was a major chief among the Apaches.

Billy rode into the camp at dusk. A young boy took him to the chief's wickiup. The family sat inside eating dinner. As Billy approached, the chief stepped outside to meet him.

"My son, White Warrior, I knew you would come." They shook hands warmly, the Indian way, hand to arm. Seesoff emerged from the wickiup and embraced Billy.

"My son, the gods have been good to you. You are big, strong, and handsome." A beautiful young girl stepped out. It was Star, Billy's sister. He moved forward, picked her up, swung her around, and held her off the ground in an embrace.

When he set Star down, Billy spoke quietly and rapidly. "I hate to rush this," he said looking intently at Seesoff. "But we need to get away from here as soon as possible." The women worked to pick up the personal items and clothing they would need.

"I will get the horses," Billy said. "Meet me in those trees outside the camp. We need to ride steady for a few hours to get off the reservation." Billy turned toward Buckskin Hat and handed him a pouch. "Father, here is three hundred dollars' worth of gold to help you with your living. Spend it carefully to avoid attention."

They said good-bye to the chief. The women walked toward the trees while Billy rode to the agency store. They never saw Buckskin Hat again. He was shipped on a railroad car to Fort Marion, Florida, in 1886 when the United States

Army moved hundreds of Apache people from their homes in San Carlos to Florida. This included over fifty of the Apache scouts who had helped the army capture Geronimo. When Billy heard the news much later he spat on the ground and pronounced the treatment "treachery."

It was nearly dark. Billy gathered the horses at the agency store and rode to the cluster of trees where the women were waiting. They mounted the horses and set off on their way in a short time. Billy planned to travel through the northern edge of the Mescal Mountains. This was to help avoid encountering traffic from Globe. After four hours of steady riding, the trio stopped to eat. They rested for two hours and then rode until late in the night. This put them well away from the reservation.

The next morning the party took a longer rest. Billy hobbled the horses in a patch of graze and put out some grain. Seesoff and Star made beds of blankets in a grove of trees. Billy found a vantage point and scanned the country that lay in the path to home. He planned to stay in the tree line when possible and away from ridgelines that could silhouette them. He figured they would be there in three to four days, depending on the weather and traffic. As long as they had a good moon and the terrain was level, they could travel at night.

The women were excellent riders and the group made good time. Staying along the edges of hills and in arroyos, Billy kept them out of sight.

On the second evening of their journey they encountered a rough-looking cowboy, apparently from a nearby ranch. The man raised his right hand in the sign of friendly greeting. Billy did the same thing with his left hand, keeping his gun hand free. The rider asked Billy what he was doing there. "We're headin' for the Green Valley area," Billy told him. "I have family and property there."

"Are you a squaw man?" asked the rider, looking at Seesoff and Star.

"No, these are sisters from my adopted family." Billy controlled his anger.

The man mused at the thought. "That young one would be a nice prize."

"You'd have to pass the judgment of this Colt," Billy said as he shifted in his saddle to free his angle for a draw.

"Hold on! I'm just funnin'," the man said as he saw Billy grow grim. He spurred his horse and moved down the trail.

"Are there more of you around here?" Billy called after him.

"No, you should have a clear trail ahead. On the road there are army units patrolling."

Billy waved in thanks. "Have a good trail," he said flatly. He watched the rider move over a rise and disappear. They rode for about a hundred yards and then Billy stopped and turned around to watch the back trail.

"What's wrong, Billy?" Seesoff asked.

"That rider was too interested in Star and he got friendly a little too quickly. We will set here a moment and take a little rest." Billy scoured the back trail and flanks. After a while, he was satisfied that the rider had moved on, and he led the party down the trail.

They began traveling during the day because the land drifted casually and the way ahead could be easily seen.

In the evenings they would sit around and talk until dark fell. When the women were settled in bed, Billy would move his position higher for a guard post. He would rest leaning against a tree or rock with a good view around the area. If intruders came in the night he would surprise them from a different position than the women.

With his Winchester cradled in his arm, Billy rested in a doze. He had trained himself to become aware and rise from a doze if there was the slightest change in ambience.

During their evening talks, Seesoff told of her life after she left the store at Verde. The war had been a disaster for her people. Crook, his army equipped with the new Springfield rifle, killed hundreds of Indians. The army moved the survivors onto the reservation at Verde and later moved them again to San Carlos. Her father had not been the same since. Buckskin Hat had been relegated to a minor role in reservation politics. Geronimo was leading uprisings among the camps. The old chiefs' voices fell on the winds of war talk and were lost.

At one of their evening talks, Billy told Seesoff and Star about their new home. They would live in a small camp of six families a short distance from the settlement. There was no chief but one man was looked upon as the leader. Billy had made arrangements with the leader for Seesoff and Star to join the camp. Billy would be close by and the women were under his protection. Any person harming the women would answer to White Warrior. Billy assured Seesoff and Star that they would be safe.

Seesoff reasoned that Billy's family would be affected by these arrangements. "Billy," she asked, "do you have a wife and family?"

"My family is the Murphys," Billy told her, looking into the low flames of the campfire. "I have lived with them since my father was killed."

"What about a wife?" Star asked.

"I have no wife," Billy responded, sounding pensive.

Seesoff sensed his mood. "What is wrong, Billy?"

Billy told them about Charlee, his history with her, and the incident in Prescott. "I'm confused about her behavior," he sighed. "I don't know if I fit in her life anymore. The soldier is probably more charming than I am. He can surely offer her a more comfortable life in more exciting places." He poked the fire with a stick and sparks shot up. "Her mother is against her being involved with me."

"Have you talked with her, Billy?" Seesoff asked. "You should give her a chance to explain and answer your questions."

"I don't know what to say to her," Billy said. "I'm angry and I feel betrayed. She has more time in Prescott. She may have decided this soldier is in her life now and there is no place for me." With this, Billy dropped the stick in his hand, said good night, and moved toward his night watch position.

"Seesoff, Billy is in love with this girl," Star said. "I wish we could see her and tell her more about him. My brother is a wonderful person. She may not be good enough for him. I hope our being part of his life now will not cause problems for him with her."

The next morning was clear and fresh. Seesoff and Star prepared breakfast while Billy scanned the country with his glass. He caught a slight movement or a reflection off of metal but was not sure. He tossed a pebble to get their attention and motioned to the women not to move and be quiet. He studied the trees and bushes ahead. There it was again, some movement about two hundred yards out. Billy was thirty yards above and to the side of the camp. He saw two men crawling behind trees and tall grass toward the camp. The intruders seemed focused on the camp and didn't know he was there.

Billy crawled higher up the hill to get a better vantage point. Using his glass, he found three horses, tied off down the trail. There could be another man flanking the camp. Scanning the glass along the hillside, Billy located the man moving toward the camp directly in his path. Billy moved down the trail to the point where he could intercept the man. Concentrating on the camp location, the man stepped from behind a pine tree and received a sharp blow to the head from the butt of Billy's Winchester. Billy judged this would hold the man for a while.

He moved over the crest of the hill and down behind the crawling men. He moved quietly up and behind the men who were panting and sweating from the work.

"Make a wrong move and I will shoot you," Billy commanded. "Put your hands above your heads and roll over, slowly." The men rolled over and found the business end of Billy's Winchester. One of the men was the rider they had met the day before. "You don't learn well," Billy said. "Unbuckle your belts and toss them behind you."

"We don't mean any harm. I wanted the boys to see that girl and offer you one hundred in gold coin for her."

"Your partner up the hill has a sore head and you're close to being shot. Do you think that girl is for sale?" Billy was disgusted. "Throw your gun belts and rifles down the hill, carefully. Stand up and walk up the hill to pick up your friend. I'm not in the mood for you to get gritty or give me any lip." Billy moved the men up the hill to the third man, who was still dazed from the blow. "Pick him up and bring him to the camp," he told the captives.

Seesoff and Star were startled to see the strangers brought into camp.

Billy said with a forced smile, "Is this the kind of problems

I'm going to have being your big brother, Star?"

She smiled sheepishly and moved beside Seesoff.

He turned to the men. "Boys, this could have been a messy situation. If I have any more problems, I will shoot you without a thought. Take off your clothes down to your long johns, including the boots."

"Our clothes?" complained one man.

Billy tightened his grip on the rifle. "Any lip and there will be another sore head." The scene amused the women.

Billy ordered, "I want you men to start walking until you are over the top of the hill. We will take your horses and clothes with us and scatter them along the way. You know where your guns are. You will find them in time. I am close to the law down in the valley. The justice of the peace is a personal friend. Don't come down there to bother these women, or anyone; I will throw you in jail."

Seesoff had made a light meal. She, Billy, and Star casually ate as they watched the three men amble and limp up the hill. Then the two women and Billy gathered their gear and rode off down the trail. Now and then, they stopped to hang the men's clothes on bushes. Within a mile they had dispersed all the gear on the trail and tied off the horses. By the time the men found all their belongings, Billy and the women would be miles away.

"What do you think of White Warrior?" Seesoff asked Star.

"It is wonderful to have a big brother like him to protect me," Star said happily.

By the middle of the next day they were approaching the Indian camp. Billy had been explaining that the new wickiup was not quite finished. Although he was not a chief, the headman, Shanto, was clearly the leader. Billy had been helping the camp little by little, by bringing food, tools, building materials, clothing, blankets, and other items as needed. Now he could depend on the Indians to help him make a home for Seesoff and Star.

As they rode into the camp, Shanto came to meet them. "Welcome, White Warrior," he said, giving a hand and arm to shake as Billy stepped to the ground.

"These are my sisters from Buckskin Hat's family," Billy said as he moved their horses abreast of Shanto's. "This is She Speaks Softly. We call her Seesoff. This is Star. All affairs concerning them will be considered by me. I look to my friend Shanto to care for and protect them in my absence." Shanto nodded his approval and they walked to the new wickiup.

The wickiup was equipped with cooking utensils and other household goods. There was Indian-style clothing made by the camp women. Billy had also brought bolts of material and tanned deerskins.

"If you need anything else, let me know," Billy said as they settled onto the floor on plush furs. "I bought these from the Murphy store." He ran his hand across the soft rugs.

Seesoff and Star were pleased with the special effort Billy and the camp had made to make them feel comfortable and welcome. "I live at the settlement a few miles away," Billy assured Star. "I will come to see you regularly. Duane Murphy, the White father who adopted me, will help when I'm away. I will bring him to see you."

After Shanto returned to his family, Billy, Seesoff, and Star talked until the night birds began to sing. The women seemed concerned about Billy leaving. "I'll be back tomorrow," he promised. Billy hugged them both long and hard. "You will be safe here. This is your home as long as you wish. The horses are yours. Just grain them, rub them down, and settle them in the corral." Resisting an urge to look back, Billy rode out of camp toward the settlement and the responsibilities awaiting him there.

# Chapter 11: Charlee Returns from Prescott

Puzzled that Billy had not written, Charlee sent another letter to Mildred asking why she had not answered the first letter. Mildred responded immediately with a letter explaining the letter that she had given Bertha weeks ago to read and then send on to Charlee.

Charlee felt thunderstruck when she read Mildred's letter. Billy must think I betrayed him, she thought to herself. She had told Mark she was in love with another man. He understood and they had parted as friends of sorts. Charlee had never felt so alone.

She was near the end of her hospital training. Charlee wanted to go home and make all this right. She wrote a letter to her father and told him the date she would leave and that she would wait in Verde for him to escort her to the settlement.

Willard Darrow hollered for joy when he learned Charlee was coming home. He read her letter aloud to Bertha. "I'm glad she is coming home," Willard said, "but I feel something's wrong. Her letter sounds stiff and cold."

Bertha sat down next to Willard and told him about Mildred's letter, the one she didn't send on to Charlee. Willard was furious, and in a feverish move, stood up and cursed. "What were you thinking? What will you say to Charlee? You could lose the love and respect of your daughter. Billy could be estranged from all of us."

"I'm sorry," Mildred said. "I thought this soldier would give her a choice between a gun-fighting scout and a polished West Point graduate. Instead of living here in this violent land, she could live in the lights and glamour of the East."

"You're here," Willard said, his voice lower. "Are you sorry you're here in this home, at this ranch? Has it been so bad that you would exile Charlee by your behavior? I resent you placing me in this position. Billy is a fine man and will develop into an outstanding citizen in this territory."

Her voice pitched high, Bertha said, "If he is so noble, why is he going up to the Indian camp regularly to see another woman?"

Willard was startled. "What do you mean? He goes up to help the camp improve."

"Some people say he has a woman up there. He is up there almost every day. That seems a lot just to help the camp."

"You have no business talking like that," Willard said quietly, "passing on rumors. If Charlee hears you've been saying these things, true or not, your relationship will be ruined." Willard rose. "This is a dark day for our family." He left the house and left Bertha crying.

Charlee left Prescott and arrived in Verde, where Willard and two escort riders met her. They set off right away on the two-day trip and arrived in the settlement at midday. Charlee told her dad she would stay at the Pierces' that night.

"Would you come to the café and have some coffee with me?" Willard asked. "I need to talk to you."

Charlee went with Willard to Murphy's. As they entered the store, Duane and Mildred greeted them. All four sat down at the table in the kitchen.

"This is not what I had in mind for our meeting, Charlee," Willard said. "As long as we are here, we might as well get all this out in the open." Willard sighed and settled back in his chair and fingered his pipe.

"Mrs. Murphy," Charlee said, "I appreciate you sending the letter." Her eyes flashed. "Dad, I resent that you and Mom didn't send the first letter."

Mumbling, Willard commented, "I didn't see the letter, Charlee. Your mom told me about it just a bit ago. But there is another circumstance we need to discuss. Gossip has it Billy is spending a lot of time in the Indian camp because he is seeing a woman."

"He what?" Charlee shrieked. "He wouldn't leave me for another girl just because of that Prescott thing! I'm telling you all, I didn't cause this. Mark kissed me! I didn't kiss him back. I explained to him I was in love with another man. That's all there is to it."

Mildred spoke up. "I understand how that could happen, Charlee, but Billy was deeply hurt. You can still talk to him and explain what happened." Mildred turned a little gray. "This thing about another woman is not what it appears. There are things about Billy we have not told anyone. He had another life before he came to us. This is his private self; it is not ours to tell."

"Where is Billy? I want to see him," Charlee said.

Duane stepped forward. "Billy is not here. He is on a scout for the army. They are chasing the Rudd Leland gang."

"Why is he doing this?" Charlee asked. "He said he was not going to continue these things."

"This is a very special circumstance," Duane said. "In his mind, Billy didn't have a choice."

"Why is this Rudd Leland so important?" Charlee demanded.

"All I will say is that Billy has his reasons," Duane said.

"Why are you people not telling me things?" Charlee paced around the room as the others watched. "Dad, do you know?"

"Charlee, I don't know the answers to these things," Willard said. "Duane, can you please explain some of this for us?"

Duane sat quietly for a moment, rolling over his thoughts. "Charlee, I would like to take you up to the Indian camp. You can find out for yourself the answers to your questions."

Charlee stood still, tears beginning to well in her eyes, "Let's go now, right now. I can't stand this. My heart hurts."

Duane loaded his wagon to take some supplies up to the camp. They would ride together.

Charlee beckoned to Willard. "I'll be home sometime tomorrow, Dad. Don't worry, we will talk then." Charlee climbed on the wagon, and she and Mr. Murphy started on the one-hour drive to the camp.

As they left behind the last building of the settlement, Duane explained to Charlee, "Things aren't always the way they seem. I want you to let this play out before you draw any conclusions."

They moved down the road, smooth and easy. Being out for some exercise exhilarated the horses. Duane had to keep a tight rein on the nice pair of blacks. He asked Charlee, "Would you like to drive for awhile?"

Charlee took the reins and asked, "Can I let them out a little? I would like some air on my face to freshen up and clear my head."

"That's fine," Duane said, "but don't let them break into a hard run. They aren't ready for it, and neither is the load."

Charlee gave some rein and the horses responded. After a quarter mile or so, she eased the horses into a calm trot. Duane seized the moment to talk more with Charlee. "Have you and Billy made a commitment to each other for marriage?"

Tears streaked her dusty face as she described her last meeting with Billy. "We were happy. Now, I don't know. Mom has allowed Billy to go out on this dangerous scout thinking I have betrayed him."

The air was cool and caused some blush on her cheeks. The conversation turned casual, mostly about the store and mining. Billy had shown interest in both.

Duane explained, "Billy has many business plans for his future."

"And for me, I hope," Charlee said.

"Maybe so," Duane nodded.

"Maybe?"

"A lot depends on you, Charlee. Your relationship with the soldier and what Billy thinks about it. Your mother's attitude toward Billy. Maybe you and your family have moved away from where his life is. Billy's an extraordinary person. He is more than people know and understand. It is not whether Billy is good enough for us, but if our world is good enough for him."

"He is good enough for me. I have loved him for years," Charlee said.

The scent of ponderosa pines freshened the sweet air. As

they approached the camp, Duane took the reins. The camp sat in a depression in the land. A soft roll of a hill provided a backdrop for the camp. A flourishing stream framed the northern edge of the camp. Duane drove the wagon into camp and headed toward a well-kept wickiup. In front of the wickiup sat Star. Duane shouted, "Hello Star, how are you today?" Star stood and smiled.

"Is this the girl Billy is seeing?" Charlee whispered.

"Yes, one of them."

"One of them!" Charlee moaned.

"Remember, let things play out Charlee."

Charlee climbed off the wagon and approached the girl. "Are you the girl that Billy True comes to see?"

"Yes," Star said.

Charlee paled at the thought of this person taking her place with Billy. From inside the wickiup came another woman. Her hair was silvering at the temple. Her face was smooth and calm. She stepped forward and asked, "May I help you?"

"Are you the woman Billy comes to see?"

"I am She Speaks Softly. Billy calls me Seesoff. I am his Indian mother. This lovely girl is his sister, Star."

"Mother, sister," Charlee stammered, "I don't understand."

Seesoff said, "You must be Charlee Rae. Billy has spoken of you warmly."

Star edged in, "You are the girl that Billy loves." With a frown she said, "He thinks you have left him and are in love with a soldier."

"Shush," Seesoff said, "Billy did not say that. He doesn't know or understand what is happening, but he's hurt and depressed about the possibility of losing you, Charlee. I am very concerned about his state of mind out on this dangerous scout."

Charlee said, "This was an incident with the soldier, not an affair. It was not my fault. I made a mistake by letting things go too far. I'm in love with Billy and want him more than anything in the world."

Charlee stood sobbing. Seesoff came to her, held her close, and said, "You will have to explain this to Billy."

"I may not get a chance to explain," Charlee said. "Why is he on this scout? Who is this Rudd Leland?"

Seesoff slid Charlee over to a place they could sit. She explained how she had met Billy and was, in practical terms, his mother for seven years. "When he was twelve," Seesoff said, "Billy's father was attacked and killed while hauling freight for the store. The man who led the attack was Rudd Leland." She sighed. "Billy has a vendetta, a mission, to kill Leland. This is why he went on this scout. The army has been driving Leland down the eastern edge of the Mazatzal Mountains. They asked him to lead the army detachment to try and trap Leland and his gang from the south. Billy left two days ago, along with two Apache scouts. Fifteen army troops went through yesterday and will catch up with Billy in about two days. The plan called for the main detachment to force Leland into a trap." She stopped abruptly.

"And Billy right in the middle of it," Charlee said. "This is so sad. For years I have poured my heart out to Billy. Now when we could be married, I may lose him if he gets killed. I'll never forgive myself if this should happen."

"There is no fault here," Seesoff said. "If this comes to an end now, you have had a love that will warm your heart forever. Love is not a place but a path. Let's hope your path with Billy lasts."

Charlee held on to Seesoff firmly for a long time. She said,

"Now I have a sister and another mother to love. This will help me in the years to come."

Seesoff, Charlee, and Star talked while Duane unloaded the wagon. The rays of dusk emerged through the trees and Duane said, "We need to get back, Charlee."

Charlee felt relieved as they left the camp. She asked Duane, "Why was this a secret?"

Duane was putting the horses into an easy trot. "Billy didn't want his life to be the source of gossip and jokes," Duane said. "He wanted to prove himself. In the early years people were hostile to Indians. Billy didn't want to be caught up in conflicts over that hostility. Things are better now. Billy has been going up to the camp regularly to take tools and materials for use in improvement. People have noticed this and put their own spin on it, such as his going up to see a woman." Duane smiled at Charlee and she shook her head and smiled back.

They arrived in the settlement at dark. Much to her surprise, Bertha and Willard were there to meet them. After their greetings, they went into Murphy's. Charlee explained all she had found out at the camp. Willard was pleased. Setting his jaw firmly he said, "I knew Billy had good character and wouldn't take up with another woman."

Charlee said, "You people have allowed Billy to go out believing I had betrayed him. If something should happen to him out there, I don't know if I could forgive you."

Bertha cried and leaned on Willard's arm. "I meant well, daughter. I wanted the best for you."

"The best for me is what I want now," Charlee said, standing straight and still. "I want Billy home safe, and if he will have me, we are going to be married soon." She looked at her mother, softened, and reached over to give her a hug and a kiss. Bertha melted into Charlee's arms and sobbed.

Willard, seeking to clear the air of the heavy wave of despair, said, "Who is that over in the corner?"

Duane smiled. "That's Billy's new dog. A rancher who was moving out of the area asked us to take him." The dog was large, with a blond coat and a smile on its face. "He had good manners and was social. His name's Ring. Billy and Ring spend a lot of time together. Charlee, you need to get acquainted with him. He is part of the family."

Charlee called Ring and he responded to her affectionately. After jostling with Charlee, Ring lay down by her feet. She scratched the fur between his ears.

"Are we staying here tonight?" Charlee asked.

"Why don't we eat and stay the night," Bertha said, seeking to keep her daughter's favor.

"That will be fine with me," said Charlee. "I can tell you and the Murphys of my experiences in Prescott, my work." She looked around. "But we need to get my luggage in from the porch." She moved away from the table to go check on the room Mildred was preparing. Ring followed along at her heels.

# Chapter 12: The Pursuit of Rudd Leland

Rudd Leland and his gang had been marauding around the territory for over ten years. His gang consisted of White outlaws and rogue Indians. The group varied between fifteen and twenty men. They attacked wagon trains, ranches, settlements, and travelers.

The army launched a campaign against Leland in 1873. Billy served as a scout with the Tenth Cavalry during this time. Billy missed an opportunity to get Leland. His shot was off target and he hit Leland in the leg.

Leland was distinctive in his dress. He wore a black long-sleeved shirt with a cross-the-chest bandoleer. He wore Apache-style pants and leggings. A foot-long pigtail fell down his back. An Apache bandana was pulled back into a headband. He sported a large bowie knife on his waistband along with a holstered Colt.

The gang roamed the wilderness areas of the Mogollon Rim, Tonto Basin, and the mountains to the south. Leland would set up base camps and work out of these, moving camps regularly. The gang would go inactive for periods of time then reappear for a planned attack.

One afternoon, Billy returned from the Indian camp and was met by an army courier with a letter from General Crook. The courier was to wait for Billy's response. Billy read the letter carefully and gave it to Duane to study.

"Dad, they want to give me a temporary commission as chief scout, with a rank of lieutenant. They want me to lead part of a campaign against Leland. They've forced him south with a pincer movement. Prescott will push from the north and northwest. Verde will come from the northeast. The Tenth Cavalry is moving and pushing Leland in front of them, south from Prescott and Verde. Leland is running hard down the eastern edge of the Mazatzals." Billy looked out the window as if he could spot Leland there. A red-tailed hawk soared past.

"The military telegraph is keeping Leland in sight with patrols and communication," he continued. "Crook has detached a special unit from the Tenth to try and trap Leland as he exits the mountains. I am supposed to find Leland and lead the detachment to trap him. The detachment has fifteen men with the new Springfield rifles. The Tenth is a Black cavalry regiment. They are great fighters. I served with them in '73 when we were chasing Leland then."

"How do you plan to do this, Billy?" Duane asked. "Leland has a tough group of fighters with him. Your detachment will have to run them and trap them when they come out of the draws. How can you do that with fifteen troopers?"

"I don't know, Dad. The troops should be here tomorrow or the next day, according to this letter. I'm going to pick up two Apache scouts at Claw Hand's camp. We'll leave tonight and scout the foothills along the Mazatzals. If we can cut trail, we'll shadow Leland until the troop catches up. We'll plan our action then."

"Billy," Duane said, "if they should turn on you before the troop arrives, we could lose all three of you." Duane was concerned about how vulnerable Billy and his scouts would be. "Can you wait until the troop comes, then plan your attack from there?"

Billy reached to pour another cup of coffee and said, "A larger group can be seen easier. Three of us can cover a large area with our glasses. Leland will be moving fast and his scouts will be running and not taking as much care as they should. If we spot them and plot their line of march, we can lay a trap and kill them."

Duane knew Billy had made up his mind because he was beginning to pack his bags and gather equipment. "Dad," Billy asked, "would you write a short response to the letter and send the courier back? He should eat before he leaves. Mom, would you pack jerky and supplies for three of us for three days? Pack three bags so we can distribute the weight. Dad, I want to borrow two of the new Springfields for the scouts. We'll need two hundred rounds of ammo for the Springfields. I will need two hundred rounds of .44s for my Winchester and Colt since they use the same cartridges. I would like to leave within an hour."

Mildred moved forward and hugged Billy. "Son, can't you wait for the troops?"

"No, I really can't. But you can help me by making sure people treat the troops with respect and dignity. A bag of your sweets for each trooper would be nice. Don't call them 'buffalo soldiers.' They don't like the name. They are troopers. I couldn't ask for better troops to be fighting with."

Mildred was working on the packing. Duane came in to help.

"Billy," Mildred asked, "are you physically and emotionally fit for this? Is Charlee on your mind to the point of affecting your judgment?"

Billy looked up from his bag. "I've been better but I'm in good physical condition. The responsibility to my troopers will keep me alert. When you see Charlee, tell her to be happy in her new life with the soldier if that's what she wants."

"Billy, you sound like you expect not to come back," Mildred pressed. "Stop thinking like that. We love you and need you in our lives, regardless of what Charlee is doing."

Billy turned and smiled, saying, "My purpose is to kill Rudd Leland. Then I expect to return to my family." Billy sat down on an easy chair in the kitchen. Ring came up to nuzzle Billy's hand to get a scratch. Billy closed his eyes for a moment to catch a little rest. Images of Charlee drifted through his mind. She drifted out of his world into a world of splendor and delight. He wasn't in her new world.

When everything was packed Billy checked his gear, with particular attention to his guns. He turned to Duane. "Dad, please tell the officer in charge to march south at a walk. We will send word where to meet down the line of march. I hope to see you within a week." Billy rode out toward the Indian camp to get his two scouts.

Duane had seen many occasions during the war when he sent men to fight, feeling he would not see them again. This feeling surged through him now.

Billy met with Chief Claw Hand to discuss the use of two warriors as scouts. He would pay the camp two horses and provide each warrior's lodge with one head of cattle. He would lend each warrior a new Springfield rifle. Claw Hand was pleased to see Billy and find warriors for him. He also told Billy his scouts had tracked a group of men moving fast and making short stops for rest and food. The scouts also noticed an increase in army activity, seemingly following the men. Billy was grateful to Claw Hand for this information.

Billy met his scouts, a sturdy pair of warriors. He gave them their supplies and guns. With a little instruction from Billy, the warriors managed their rifles well. As they were preparing to leave the camp, Claw Hand asked, "How is my daughter White Fawn? Do you have sons yet?"

"White Fawn is fine and we have no children," Billy managed.

The three scouts rode down the east side the Mazatzals, scanning the mountain passes and canyons. Rudd had to move downward to save his horses. When they hit the flatland they could disperse, steal fresh horses, and disappear. Billy determined they would have to attack Leland before the gang dispersed. This would be at the mouth of the canyon or an opening to the flatland.

With the spottings they received from Claw Hand, they could project likely locations. They picked three lookout stations. They would cover the country from the lookout points, meet again, and repeat the process until they located Leland.

One of the Apache scouts located Leland's column in a shallow, long canyon leading to the flatlands. The three met and discussed the likely route Leland would take. The long canyon went for about fifteen miles. The gang was bedded down for a rest period. Billy would have to contact the troops and lead them to where Leland was in the canyon.

Billy left the scouts to watch Leland's gang while he located the troops. They should be within a few miles to the north.

Billy had ridden about five miles when he spotted the troops. He slowed to a walk and met the troops led by a

White officer. He recognized the soldier he had seen with Charlee on the porch in Prescott. Billy felt a sick feeling in his stomach. Billy greeted the lieutenant and introduced himself. Mark edged forward on his horse and shook Billy's hand firmly.

Mark said, "I have heard a lot about you from many circles. General Crook thinks highly of your skills as a scout. Others recognize your ability as a gunfighter." The men's eyes met momentarily in silent recognition.

"We need to move faster now to meet my scouts," Billy said. "We have located Leland near the head of that long canyon." Billy pointed and traced the canyon with his hand. "He has stopped for a rest. We need to ride down to meet the scouts."

The troop rode at a trot for a few miles until they met the scouts. The scouts reported that Leland had bedded down, with horses unsaddled. There were eighteen men in the gang.

Billy noticed a soldier he had known in the past. He rode over and called, "Sergeant Hooks."

The soldier moved closer and smiled, saying, "White Warrior, you have grown. It's been, what? Five years since we chased Rudd before?" They shook hands firmly and the sergeant briskly saluted. They had been told that the scout they were meeting was an officer.

"That's not necessary. I'm glad to see you, Sergeant. I see they finally made you top soldier. It's about time. This could be a messy fight. Take care of yourself."

The troop dismounted and was told to rest. Billy, Mark, and Sergeant Hooks sat down to discuss tactics.

"If we don't surprise them we will lose a lot of men and still not get Leland," Billy said. "We're here to kill them. We can't let them get behind us. Do you have a plan, Lieutenant? Sergeant?"

Mark said, "We don't have time for extensive planning. Do you have something, Billy? If so, let's have it."

"The canyon they're in is about a thousand feet deep and shallows out as it nears the flats," Billy described. "Leland sets up his column, single file along the bottom where it's easy going. There are two scouts out in front, one on each side. There are two more scouts abreast of the column, one on each side. This column design tells me he believes he has enough lead on the army following him. He does not have a rear guard. We can't let them disperse. We have to drive them into our guns. We can't think to capture anyone. They can't be bypassed alive; they would fire on us from our rear."

Mark interrupted. "We will have to split our troops—half to chase, the other half to trap. We have fifteen troopers, two scouts, and you, Billy. The trapping group will be in serious danger. If the chasing group is late, Leland's entire gang will hit and overwhelm the trapping group before they can get support."

"You're right, Lieutenant. The chasing group must hit and chase the gang, killing as they go. They can't let some slip by or leave wounded able to attack from behind. I suggest that Sergeant Hooks and I take five troopers and set up a firing line near the mouth of the canyon. The gang should be at full gallop when they come under our guns. It's hard shooting from a running horse. They won't be accurate. We should hold them long enough for the chase group to hit from behind. We will have them in a crossfire. We need to kill Rudd Leland or he will form another gang. You will have ten men pushing from behind. I don't think the gang will try to climb the sides of the canyon, too steep. They may split up if they get to the opening of the canyon. We don't have enough men to run them down." Billy looked around to make sure the men were following his reasoning. He continued.

"Lieutenant, your men need to slip in behind the gang's column and form about a one-hundred-yard line across the canyon floor. Move forward until you make contact. Start the running fight at the gallop. Slow down only to keep them in front or kill stragglers. Your men need to understand this is a killing raid, not a capture effort. If you are too far behind them, they will overrun us and break into the open. We don't have enough men to be successful in a long running fight. Their horses should break down and tire before ours. That should keep you close to them. Our scouts will wear a white bandana on their heads so the troopers won't mistake them for a gang member. Is this plan reasonable to you?"

Sergeant Hooks spoke. "If the lieutenant is late, the seven of us are casualties. This is a risky plan, but it has a good chance to work."

"The plan is sound," Mark agreed. "Are five troopers enough for the lower group? Maybe we should bring one or two more down from the chasing group?"

"The most critical part of the strategy," Billy explained, "is to keep the gang in the front, not spilling over and creating a crossfire on the troopers. Once the fighting starts, the gang members will be shooting backward, while the troopers have a better target. By the time the flow hits us below, the gang's horses will be tired and will be beginning to balk and slow. That's when our firing line will pour bullets into them. If things work well, the gang will be dead in a short time."

"Let's go with it. How about you, Sergeant?"

Hooks smiled. "It's a good day for fighting and dying."

Lieutenant Mark Evans divided the men and assigned the troopers to the groups. Each group took one of the Apache scouts. The groups met to get the plan explained.

"Lieutenant," Billy said, "you should leave now and move into the canyon well above the gang. When you are in position, move down the canyon at a walk until you engage. The troopers should fire at will, leaving nothing alive behind. We will set up the firing line at the mouth of the canyon. We will start firing as soon as the first of the gang breaks into view. This should keep them down at the bottom of the canyon. If they turn up, it will outflank the firing line before we could change position. We could not contain them and would lose any advantage."

The two groups moved toward their position. Billy rode abreast of Mark and said, "Good luck, Mark. I hope you and Charlee will be happy together." Billy spurred out at a gallop to meet his men.

Mark shouted after Billy, "You have things wrong, Scout." The wind snatched his words away.

Billy and his troopers rode steadily to the mouth of the canyon. Sergeant Hooks and Billy set the firing line, one man every ten yards. They positioned themselves to look down on the floor of the canyon.

Hooks said, "Billy, see that small butte on the right? They should round the butte and come under our guns. If they should break up the butte, they will be on our flank. That would be serious for us."

Billy looked at Hooks and said, "Let's hope for Lady Luck to be with us." Billy took a position up from the butte. Hooks took the first position in the firing line.

Mark led his men up the hill above the canyon. The Apache scout located Leland's column moving down the canyon in the pattern Billy had described. The troopers moved up the hill and dropped down four hundred yards behind Leland's column. Mark moved the chase group slowly in behind the gang. The troopers spread out as planned. They moved at a brisk walk to close behind the column.

They were within fifty yards of the column when they were discovered. A shout of warning from the rear of the column brought a volley of shots from the troop. Several gang members fell from their horses. The troop charged at the gallop, firing rapidly with their new Springfield rifles.

The column spread out as they galloped down the canyon. As a gang member broke up the side of the canyon he was met with a volley of shots from the troopers. Frightened and scrambling horses obstructed the chasing troopers.

The chase was falling behind the pace. Mark led some troopers around the congestion to close on fleeing gang members. Mark thought that too many of the gang would hit the trapping group.

Billy and the trapping group were standing ready to confront the retreating gang. Their horses were tied a short distance behind the firing line. The troopers could rapidly mount and pursue. Billy was mounted and stationed above the butte. He had taken his spare Colt from the pummel bags and had put it in his waistband. The troopers would start shooting from a kneeling position and change to standing as the need to move developed.

The gunfire from the canyon increased and became louder as the battle progressed. Billy checked down the firing line. The troopers were ready and determined. Billy thought how lucky he was to have the Tenth Cavalry. They were great fighters and would not break.

The noise became deafening. Suddenly five riders burst into view and turned up the butte to the flank of the firing line. This was what they had feared.

Billy spurred his horse down the butte right at the

oncoming riders. The troopers were awestruck as Billy charged into the jaws of the attack. His Colts blazed as his charge turned the group back down toward the bottom of the canyon. Two gang members fell before Billy's guns. Another slumped over and hung to his horse's neck. Billy went down, taking a shot to the side of his chest. He rolled over on his knees and kept firing.

As more gang members charged down the bottom of the canyon, the firing line erupted into volleys of rifle shots. Gang members fell. Mark, leading the chase group, broke onto the scene and provided vicious crossfire.

Suddenly it was over. Two gang members were standing with their hands up. Others were down—dead and dying. Mark rode up to Billy, who was standing by his horse getting bandages. Mark shouted, "Billy, you're hit," and leapt off his horse to help Billy with the bandages.

Billy said, "Put the compress on the wound, wrap it around, and tie it off." Billy added, "Mark, Rudd and one man got over that rise in the bottom. I know where he will go. That way opens up into a little arroyo that empties back into this canyon down below. We have to get him. I'm taking Hooks and a scout with me to cut them off below." As he was talking he was loading his guns and getting his Winchester from the scabbard.

Mark said, "Billy, you're hit. Can you do this?"

Billy smiled. "By your leave, sir, Sergeant Hooks and scout, on me." The three rode off down the canyon at a hard gallop.

Within a mile and a half the canyon merged into the arroyo. Billy said, "Scout, you ride down to the end and see if they got past us. We will wait here. Their horses should be spent and will be slow getting to this point."

Billy and Hooks concealed themselves in some spruce

trees on the edge of the arroyo. The arroyo was about fifty yards wide at this point. Within a short time Leland and his man rode down the arroyo. Billy told Hooks, "Shoot the other man but leave Rudd to me."

One shot from Hooks dropped the man. Leland lurched his horse behind a tree. Billy shouted, "Rudd Leland, this is Billy True. You are cornered and will die here. I'm asking you to come out and fight me hand to hand, Apache style, knife only. If you win, they will take you back for trial. Otherwise you will die here."

Rudd shouted back, "Why have you been hounding me, Scout? I don't know you."

"Eight years ago your gang killed my father during a raid on some freight wagons. You cut his throat and scalped him."

"You say they will take me back for trial when I kill you?" Rudd shouted.

"I said, 'If you win.' That's still in doubt." Billy turned to Hooks, "If he gets past me, tie him up good and march him to the lieutenant. If he attempts a break, kill him."

"Billy, you're wounded and bleeding," Hooks said in a low voice. "Are you sure you're fit for this?"

"I don't know. This is the last chance I will get."

Billy stepped out from behind the tree and walked toward Rudd. They stopped fifteen feet apart.

Seeing Billy's wound, Rudd said, "You will get no quarter from me because of that."

"Don't need any," Billy said sternly.

The two fighters circled each other, moving closer. Billy lunged and swiped at Rudd's knife hand. Rudd swung back and barely missed Billy's leg. Billy determined he was faster than Rudd. His wound weakened him, though. This would have to finish quickly.

The sparring continued for a few minutes. Billy made a thrust at Rudd's arm, missed, and Rudd lunged forward and drove his knife deep into Billy's left thigh. Billy grabbed Rudd's knife hand, and with the knife still in his leg, lunged forward and drove his knife deep in Rudd's chest just below the breastbone. With a side swipe with his knife Billy expanded the cut into the liver. Billy pulled back. Rudd fell over on his side, coughing blood. Billy pulled Rudd's knife from his leg and blood began to flow. Rudd rolled over on his back and gazed at Billy, "You killed me, Scout." Life began to drain from his face.

Billy turned to Hooks and motioned him over. Hooks and the scout came riding over. Billy told Hooks to get a compression bandage for his leg. Billy took his knife and walked toward Rudd.

Rudd groaned, "You're not going to scalp me are you?"

Billy strode toward Rudd. "You scalped my father."

Rudd screamed, "Please don't scalp me."

Billy stepped over Rudd and grabbed his pigtail. Lifting Rudd's head he ran his knife around the braided hair and removed it. He walked away.

Sergeant Hooks said, "Did you scalp him, Billy?"

Billy said, "No, I just took the hairpiece and a little hide. He died thinking I was scalping him." He handed the hairpiece to Hooks and told him, "Give it to the lieutenant. He can then give it to General Crook as a gift. It's a special gift from Billy True."

Billy sat on the ground. He and Hooks bandaged his leg and put a fresh bandage on his side. "Sergeant," Billy said, "I don't think I can ride. I lost a lot of blood. I may not make it."

Sergeant Hooks told the scout to get two long poles and some smaller ones to build a travois to carry Billy. Hooks firmed up the bandages. In a short time they were on their way out of the canyon and up the valley. The scout went ahead to report to Mark.

The battle scene was quiet when the scout reported to Mark. Mark gave instructions to a trooper to ride to the settlement and report to Captain Murphy. The trooper rode at a trot to save the horse. The settlement was about twenty miles away.

It was turning to dusk as the trooper rode into the settlement. He asked for Captain Murphy and was directed to the store. Duane was getting ready to close the store when the trooper came in.

"I'm looking for Captain Murphy," he said.

Duane motioned to the nearest chair. "Sit down, trooper," he said. "You look bushed. Mildred, bring some water and coffee." After the trooper was refreshed he told of the battle and that the troop killed or captured all the gang members.

Duane looked at his hands, "Your casualties?" he asked.

The trooper said, "One trooper dead and two wounded. Billy went down with some serious wounds. Sergeant Hooks and an Apache scout are bringing him in on a travois.

Mildred bit her lip to control her tears. "I'll go get Dr. Pierce and Charlee," she said.

She grabbed a shawl and ran to the doctor's office. She found Dr. Pierce reading and Charlee washing up for bed.

Mildred told the news. The Pierce home erupted with alarm. Charlee and Dr. Pierce grabbed their bags and headed to the store. Dr. Pierce barged through the door with Charlee on his heels.

"The troop has destroyed Rudd Leland and his gang," Duane said without a hello. "As you might expect, Billy played a major role in the fight. He has some serious wounds and is being brought in on a travois."

"Should we go to meet them?" Charlee asked.

Duane shook his head. "The best I can figure he is about an hour away. If we go to him, there is no place to work. By the time you get there and back, he could be here. I suggest you wait here."

Dr. Pierce agreed. "Charlee, we need to get the office ready to meet two wounded troopers and Billy."

"He can't die before I get to talk to him," Charlee moaned.

"There is no reason to believe he is going to die," Dr. Pierce admonished. "Charlee, think like a doctor, not with your heart but with your head."

"Duane," Charlee asked, "Can you ride to meet them and tell Billy I'm waiting here for him?"

"I'm on my way," Duane said, as he headed to the stables to saddle his horse.

"I'll start getting a large amount of food ready," Mildred said. "We will have to get help from the ranches. Have one of the Blake boys ride to the closest ranches for help. The Darrows will come in to help. Those fighters were out there protecting us. They need us now."

Duane had been out about thirty minutes when he met Sergeant Hooks and the scout. "We are ready for you in town. How is Billy?"

Hooks said, "He doesn't look good. He is in and out of consciousness. We have stopped most of the bleeding."

Duane got off his horse and walked alongside the travois. "Billy, are you awake?"

"Hello, Dad," Billy said. "Why are you out here? We will be home in a short time."

"Charlee was worried about you and sent me out to tell you she was waiting."

Billy said weakly, "Are you sure it's me and not Mark? He is back cleaning up the mess we made of the Leland gang." Billy dropped off to sleep.

Duane told Sergeant Hooks where Dr. Pierce's office was. He led them down the street and stopped at the office. Hooks and Duane dismounted to take Billy into the office. Dr. Pierce and Charlee rushed out to assist. Charlee burst into tears as they put Billy on a table. Billy moaned and stirred from his unconsciousness to see Charlee close to his face.

"Hello, Charlee," Billy said.

Charlee placed her face against his cheek. "Billy. I love you so much."

Billy said through his delirium, "I thought you left me, Charlee."

"No, oh no," Charlee wept as she kissed his mouth and cheeks. "I will never leave you. I have loved you for years. You're my one and only." A tear flowed from the corner of Billy's eye as he drifted off to sleep.

Embarrassed by the scene, Dr. Pierce said, "Charlee, let's get his clothes off; he has blood all over. Will it bother you to do this? Should I get Duane to help?"

"No," Charlee said, "I'll have to see him to help with his wounds. We can drape him with a sheet as we cut off his clothes."

"Good Lord," Dr. Pierce said. "How could he fight with these wounds? What a warrior!"

They examined his chest wound and found a bullet had hit his left breast and followed a rib around. The bullet had broken two ribs and exited behind the armpit. The bandage slowed the bleeding but some sutures were needed.

Billy's blood pressure was low. He needed liquids to bring the pressure up. Charlee left the table to get clean bandages.

When she returned, Dr. Pierce said, "Charlee, stay close. When you leave he worsens; when you come back he begins to rally. Stay close and talk to him. Make sure he knows you are here."

Charlee held and kissed his hand. "I love you, Billy," Charlee said as she moved to clean his chest wound.

Dr. Pierce was examining the wound in the left thigh. It was bleeding slowly. "No arteries involved," Dr. Pierce said. "This is a deep wound. Let's put pressure until we can suture. Charlee, let's bathe him with a carbolic acid solution to help kill the germs."

Charlee cleaned Billy's upper body while Dr. Pierce worked on the lower body. When they finished, they discussed the suturing that would be needed. "He's much stronger now," the doctor said. "We could use some chloroform to make him sleep for the suturing. Let's talk to Billy and see how he feels about the anesthesia. We could use a local anesthesia, it might be enough."

Billy was awake, listening to the discussion. Billy said, "Let's get on with it. Use the local stuff."

Outside, the troop was coming into the settlement. One trooper was over a saddle and, because there was no room at the doctor's, was taken to the jail and placed on a cot. Duane Murphy met with Mark and Sergeant Hooks.

"You can put your horses in the corrals across the street," Duane told them. "You can unsaddle and rub down there. We have arranged for grain and other feed there. You can house the troopers in the recreation center, up the street and on the left. There are latrines in back with water and basins for washing. When you are ready we will set up a mess line for feeding. The women have been preparing food for hours. I don't know what it is but it will be good and plenty of it."

Mark told Hooks to assign troopers to assist at the corrals and the rest at the recreation hall. "Put a man in charge at each site," he added. "I want you with me to help make a report to Captain Murphy."

"A report to me is not necessary, Lieutenant."

"I want to make sure we get the report correct," Mark insisted. "Hooks was present at some action where I wasn't. I want as many people to hear the report as possible. I want the settlement to know what these troopers did."

Mildred volunteered to record the report as the men talked. Bertha and Willard arrived from the ranch. Other ranchers gathered to hear the news.

Mark described the strategy designed by Billy and executed by him and Hooks. "'The troopers executed the plan perfectly,' write that down," Mark told Mildred.

Charlee came in the door to report on how Billy was doing. "We finished putting thirty-one sutures in two major wounds. We gave him something to make him sleep. Dr. Pierce has gone over to see the two troopers who were wounded. We were told the wounds were not serious. Mrs. Pierce is sitting with Billy."

Charlee caught Mark's eye and went over to shake his hand. "Hello, Mark, I'm glad you're not hurt," she said.

"Thank you," Mark said. "I think Billy took enough for all of us."

Charlee smiled and nodded to Mark.

Mark continued his report. "The chase group engaged the enemy from a walk into a full gallop. They were caught by surprise. The troopers kept them hemmed in. The outlaws were under heavy fire from the troopers. The chase went for about three miles. We broke into the canyon mouth where the trap group was giving fire. The enemy was about wiped out at the time. Sergeant Hooks, would you report what happened on your end?"

Hooks said, "The enemy came upon us and broke up over a butte and threatened our right flank. The scout rode directly into the enemy, his guns firing rapidly. He killed two of them and wounded another. They turned down toward the bottom of the canyon and were met by the full force of our firing line. Billy fell, having taken a hit to his chest. He rose to his knees and kept firing. I have not seen anything like it in my career. He turned the enemy's column back away from our flank. In my opinion he saved many lives; this was at the risk of his own life. I think he believed he was going to die today."

Charlee began to sob. Mildred went to Charlee and comforted her, "Billy's okay now, Charlee."

"Did he not care because of me?" Charlee said.

"I don't know."

Mark continued, "Our chasing group broke onto the scene about the time Billy turned the column. Our troopers had them in a crossfire. Most of the killing took place here. The enemy went down except for two who dropped their guns and raised their hands. It was at this time Billy mounted his horse and told me that Leland and another rider slipped over a little rise and were heading down another canyon. Although he was wounded he said he was going down the canyon to cut Leland off below. I told him he should not because he was wounded. Billy took Sergeant Hooks and an Apache scout and started down the canyon."

"Mark," Charlee cried, "why didn't you stop him?"

Mark asked for a recess from the meeting and motioned Charlee to come over out of earshot of the others. Mark said, "Billy knew he was hit hard but he seemed not to care. He rode next to me as we moved to our positions before the fight. He wished us happiness and rode off at a gallop. I shouted to him that he was wrong, but I don't think he heard me because of the noise."

Charlee shed more tears as she went back to the group. "I'm sorry. This is very hard for me. Most of you know I love Billy very much." Many nodded their heads and smiled.

Mark went on to say, "Sergeant Hooks witnessed the next stage of the report."

Hooks rose and said, "Billy led us down the canyon to where he thought Leland and the other man would come out. In a few minutes the two rode into the open. Billy ordered me to shoot the man but leave Leland to him. I killed the man and Billy yelled to Leland to come out and fight him Apache style, with a promise he would live to go to trial if he could get past Billy. They came together on foot."

Charlee cried out, "Why didn't you stop him, Sergeant? You knew he was wounded!"

"Miss Charlee," Hooks said, "he had a personal reason to want to kill Leland. Billy is a warrior. If he failed, he would die a warrior's death by personal combat."

Charlee sobbed as she left and walked toward Dr. Pierce's office.

Hooks cleared his throat and continued. "Billy killed Leland in a hand-to-hand fight. He motioned us over and told me he couldn't ride. We bandaged him as best we could. We built a travois to carry him and headed for the settlement. I will never see another fighter like Billy."

The group was clearly stunned. Mildred was wiping her tears as she managed to write the transcript.

Mark continued the report. "The troopers cleaned up the battle area. They gathered identification from the men and buried them where they fell. The troopers searched the line of the combat path, finding and burying bodies. They rounded up stray horses and tied them for leads. They put themselves in order and began the ride to the settlement. This is the end of the military report. I will complete the rest at the end of our stay."

Bertha went to Mildred and said, "Would you go with me over to see Charlee? She needs some support now and she is not too happy with me. Maybe you could smooth the waters for me."

Mildred was ready to get away from the stress of the meeting and was happy to go with Bertha. "Let's take Ring. He might make Billy and Charlee feel better."

They walked up the street and knocked on the office door. Mrs. Pierce answered and greeted the ladies. "Billy had a light supper and is sleeping. Charlee is in her room, on her bed crying. She has had a very hard time with this situation with Billy."

Mildred said to Bertha, "Let's go and give her some hugs and kisses." They knocked on Charlee's door and met her as she stepped out. Tears were still flowing and she sobbed when she saw them. She went to her mother and held her close.

"Mom," Charlee said, "can you believe the physical and mental pain Billy felt and still fought the way he did? I love him so much." Ring nuzzled Charlee's hand and was greeted by a little scuffle and a hug.

They heard Billy say something from his room. They went to see what he wanted. Ring went to Billy's side and whined. He had not seen Billy for a few days and was happy to feel his hand on his head.

"Hi, Ring," Billy said and pulled him up for a little hug.

Charlee said, "Billy, we shouldn't have Ring in here because of infection. I'll take him out in the other room and tell him to stay." She took Ring to the other room, left him there, and came back to Billy.

Billy said, "You ladies need to come a little closer. I have something to say." Charlee came in close and gave Billy a little kiss on the cheek. "I have loved Charlee for years. There for a while I thought I had lost her."

"I wouldn't leave you." Tears swelled in Charlee's eyes.

Billy placed his right hand on Charlee's cheek and said, "I don't think you should cry now, Charlee. This is a happy moment for us. Mrs. Darrow, I want to tell you now that I want to marry Charlee as soon as I'm healed up. I want you to tell Willard. Please take this as a request for permission. You need to know we will be married regardless of your permission. That's all right with you, Charlee?"

Charlee leaned forward, embraced Billy gingerly, and said, "Of course it is. I want to give you the sons the shaman and Claw Hand asked you about."

Charlee's statements startled Mildred and Bertha. Bertha said, "In proper time, Charlee."

Charlee said, "Oh, I know, Mother. Billy's very proper!"

Mildred said with a deep breath, "It's time for us to leave. Thank you for telling us how you feel."

Charlee ushered the women out of the room. "Mom," she insisted, "tell Dad what Billy and I want. It's time for everyone to know and accept this relationship. Mildred, we need you and Duane to give us your blessing. It is important to Billy and me that our parents are giving us support."

Mildred said, "Charlee, I know I can speak for Duane. We would be delighted to have you in our family."

Charlee choked back a tear. "Thank you, Mildred, that

means a lot to me."

On the way back to the store Mildred said to Bertha, "You and Willard need to make a special effort to build your relationship with Billy. It is time for all of us to support these two."

Bertha said, "I suppose it will go the way they want. Willard will support the marriage and so will I."

Mildred accepted Bertha's response as meaning things would go well for Billy and Charlee. "We'll leave Ring with Charlee," Mildred said. "He will comfort both of them." The women went into Murphy's store to find the meeting finished. Duane and Mark were discussing when the troopers would leave.

The next day the troopers had cleaned the bivouac area and made ready to move out. Mark had met with Duane to discuss the report he would submit to General Crook. He requested a voucher be sent to Prescott headquarters for reimbursement of costs incurred by the troops.

"We'll absorb any costs," Duane said. "I'm going to lend you my two-seat springboard wagon and horses to carry your wounded. Your Verde commander can send the wagon back or we'll pick it up on our next trip."

Mark went over to see Billy and Charlee. Mrs. Pierce greeted him. Then Charlee came out and offered her hand. "Hello, Mark, nice of you to come." She took him in to see Billy. Dr. Pierce had just finished treating and bandaging the wounds.

"Hello, Mark," Billy said, "Are you on your way out?"

"Yes," said Mark," I want you to know there was nothing between Charlee and me. She loves you and always has. You two have a good life." Mark bowed, "Billy, it was an honor to serve with you."

Mark turned and left, with Charlee showing him out. On the way Mark touched her hand and whispered, "I still love you, Charlee."

Charlee said, "I know. I'm sorry."

Mark went to talk to Duane. "The troop wants to salute Billy. With your permission, sir," Mark said. Duane nodded.

As he mounted Mark ordered, "Come about right in line." The troop lined up in front of the Pierces' house.

Duane went into the office and told Billy what the troop wanted. "How will I do this?" Billy asked.

Charlee said, "It's time to get you up anyway. We will use the wheelchair." They moved Billy to the chair and Charlee rolled him out on the porch.

Sergeant Hooks shouted, "Troop attention!"

Billy asked Charlee and Duane to get him up. "No, Billy, stay seated," Charlee said, her hand on his shoulder.

Billy smiled. "I'm coming up with or without the help of White Fawn." And he rose.

Billy addressed the troop and in the loudest voice he could muster. "If I go into battle again, I would be proud to have you with me."

Sergeant Hooks commanded the troop, "For you and your lady, troop salute." The troop made a snappy hand salute and dropped their hand on "two."

Billy was moved by the honor and sat down to watch the troop ride north out of the settlement. He sat there, with Charlee holding his hand, until the troop was out of sight.

Charlee said with a laugh, "Calling me White Fawn is not going to get obedience all the time, White Warrior." She settled him back in the chair and added in a more serious tone, "Billy, I hope there will be no more battles for you, or for any of us."

114

# Chapter 13: Charlee Starts the Clinic

In October 1879, Dr. Pierce left the settlement to move to Cottonwood. This created some problems. Charlee had to stay longer in the settlement to do "sick calls" for the area. Seesoff and Star decided to help Charlee in the clinic. The women could also help in Murphy's store. They would come into the settlement from the camp regularly.

Charlee had organized the clinic and inventoried surgical tools and medications. Fees were set with the ability-to-pay factor. As patients came in they had to adjust to having Charlee treat them and to having Indians helping.

One day a rancher named Trae Smith came in with an ax wound on his leg. He let Charlee look at the wound but made a scene when Seesoff came to help. "Get that Indian out of here," he hollered.

Charlee stepped back and said, "Trae Smith, if you don't want to lose that leg, you will let us help. If she doesn't help, I don't work. Make up your mind."

Smith grumbled but said okay.

Charlee examined the leg. "This is infected," she said with

a frown, "and partial healing has the infection trapped inside. I will have to open it up and clean it out. Trae, this could be painful. I would like to give you some chloroform so you can sleep."

Trae said, "I'm afraid to sleep. I might die."

Charlee said in a kindly way, "You won't die; it will be easy for you." Seesoff got the chloroform and a gauze mask, and everything else ready. Trae was fearful and nervous about Seesoff's presence. He had inherited a set of everyday prejudices but was a good and righteous man. A fear of the unknown was a problem for him. Seesoff spoke softly to him to calm him. She started putting drops of chloroform on the mask she had placed over his mouth and nose.

Seesoff said, "Trae, listen to the birds chirping out there. Remember how they sound. Think of nice things, a warm woman or a smiling child."

Trae slipped off to sleep. Charlee took a scalpel and opened the wound. Pus and blood drained out. She took a syringe and purged the wound. She wiped the wound with carbolic acid to kill germs. Charlee placed a muslin drain at the lower end of the wound to drain while it healed. She sutured the wound down to the drain. The wound was then bandaged.

Seesoff removed the mask and gently talked to Trae as he awoke. The first thing he saw was Seesoff's attractive and kind face.

He said in his haze, "Are you an angel? Am I dead?"

Charlee smiled as Seesoff wiped Trae's face with a damp, cool cloth. He looked around to get his bearings.

"Is everything okay?" Trae said, looking intently at Seesoff.

"You will need to stay here a couple of hours," Charlee said. "We will get you something light to eat. You need to come back in a few days for me to check the leg."

"Thank you, Charlee," Trae said.

Charlee responded, "Isn't there someone else to thank, Trae?"

"Oh yes," Trae said, "Thank you, miss."

"Her name is Seesoff," Charlee said. "Isn't she lovely?"

Trae stared at Seesoff and made no comment. She smiled and went on cleaning the area.

Charlee said, "Seesoff, you stay and keep Trae comfortable. I'm going over to see Mildred. I'll be back with some food for Trae."

Charlee walked toward the Murphys' store. She marveled at the nice autumn weather. Some gladioli and sunflowers still blossomed. The air was fresh and cool. The sky was blue with scattered white clouds billowing interesting shapes. She felt good as she entered Murphy's place.

"Hello, Charlee," Mildred said as she approached. "Give me a hug."

"Thanks, Mom," Charlee replied as she sat down at a table. "Where is Billy today?"

Mildred said, "He's out scouting around. He took his Sharps and a gold pan. He will have a full day and hopefully come back with a deer and a poke of gold dust."

"How is Star doing?"

Mildred responded, "Fine, if we can keep the young men from hovering around. My, she is lovely. She does very well in the store. She stocks well and cleans everything in sight. She hasn't started helping people yet. That will come, as she gets more comfortable. How are you, Charlee?"

"I'm fine," she said and described her treatment of Trae's leg. She also told Mildred about Trae's attitude toward Seesoff.

Mildred said, "People will get used to the women as time

goes by. Duane is happy to have Star to help in the store. I think this will work out for the women."

Seesoff entered the store to say a woman had come in to report that her child and family members were sick.

Charlee said, "Seesoff, you get some food for Trae. I'll go over and see the woman." She was thinking it would be a nice day to go riding with Billy.

Charlee went into the clinic and met Elisabeth Johnson. Mrs. Johnson lived on a small ranch in the hills southeast of the settlement. The woman was very plain and unkempt. Charlee said, "May I help you, Mrs. Johnson?"

"My family has been sick for a month. I don't know what's wrong. It's mainly my girl. She stays in bed all the time."

Charlee said, "You say your whole family? How many are there?"

Elisabeth, forming tears, said, "My husband, two children, and me."

"What is your main complaint?"

"Nothing really," the woman said with her eyes lowered. "I dropped a flat iron on my toe yesterday and it's very painful. It will get better."

Charlee said, "Sit down and put your foot up." Charlee noticed that Elisabeth was dirty, her feet and legs caked with dirt smudges. The nail on the injured toe had turned black from bleeding underneath.

Charlee said, "I will have to wash your foot before I can work on the toe. You need to remember that dirt has germs that can make you sick." She cleaned the foot with soap and water.

After the cleaning Charlee examined the toe. "The blood is trapped under the nail. That's causing the pain. I'm going to make a hole in the nail and let the blood out. It will hurt for a while. Is that okay with you, Elisabeth?"

Elisabeth said, "Yes, Charlee. But will it hurt bad?"

"Yes, it will hurt badly while I'm boring into the nail and pressing the blood out."

Charlee took her scalpel and turned it as she was pressing. This bored a hole in the nail. When blood came through the hole, Charlee squeezed the blood from under the nail. It was over in just a few minutes. Elisabeth groaned with relief as the pain subsided.

Elisabeth said, "Thank you, Charlee. I'm here with my husband. Could you come up to my house and see my girl?"

"Yes I can. It will have to be tomorrow. I need to bring my assistant and Billy will come as an escort." She looked Mrs. Johnson in the eye. "My assistant is an Indian."

Elisabeth shook her head. "My husband doesn't like Indians."

"If she doesn't come, neither do I," Charlee said. "You go out and ask your husband, and come back and tell me what he says." Elisabeth went to talk with her husband about Seesoff coming along.

She came back. "It's okay if she stays outside," she reported.

"That's enough of this stuff." Charlee went out. "Mr. Johnson, do you want me to help your family?"

"Yes, Charlee."

"I need the help of my assistant. You need to change your attitude about Indians. She is a nice person and can help."

Johnson was surprised by Charlee's tenacity. "Well, if you need her that much it will have to do."

"Thank you, sir." Charlee was boiling mad. The breeze of the autumn day cooled her down as she walked to the office. She told Elisabeth they would see her the next day.

119

Charlee washed the table down with carbolic acid. She went into the other room to see how Trae was doing. He was up, dressed, and finishing his meal.

"How much do I owe, Charlee?" he asked.

"Fifteen dollars would be customary, but whatever you can pay."

Trae said, "It was well worth it with all the attention I'm getting." He gave Charlee fifteen dollars in coin. "Thank you, and thank you too, Miss Seesoff."

Charlee and Seesoff smiled as they left the office. "I think we did some good things here today."

Seesoff said, "He was kind of nice when he cooled down."

Billy returned to the settlement early in the evening. He had harvested a deer and cut it up in three sections. One section was taken to the Indian camp, one to the gold camp, and one home. He had gone to one of his favorite placer gold areas and panned about a thousand dollars' worth.

It had been a very productive day for Billy but he longed to see Charlee. He went over to see her and was met by Charlee vaulting up around his neck. She gave him a big kiss and said, "I love you, Billy."

"That was nice, Charlee, thank you for the kiss." He turned to Seesoff. "Hi, Seesoff. What kind of day did you ladies have?" Charlee explained the sessions with Trae and Elisabeth. Seesoff asked Billy to go with them to the Johnsons' the next day.

Charlee said, "We may have to spend most of the day. I fear the place will need cleaning."

Billy said, "Should I get a supply of staples from the store to take up?"

"That would be nice, but we don't want to show them until we see there is a clear need. We don't want them to feel badly about receiving help. Have Mildred pack us a big lunch. We don't know when we will be back."

"I'll go over and ask Mom about the lunch." Billy walked over to the Murphys' and gave Mildred a big hug.

"Billy," said Mildred, "you go in and change your clothes and wash up. You have deer residue on you."

"Okay, Mom. We will need a big lunch for three tomorrow. We are going up to the Johnson ranch to help the family with their health issues."

Mildred smiled, "I'm going to charge you for my food and labor."

"Thanks. Put it on my account at the store." Billy went over to the store. "Dad, here is some dust. I would like you to weigh it and put it on my account. Be sure to pay off my debts to you. Charlee and I need to start paying our way. We have to keep track of our spending with renting your house, staying in the hotel, and building a house."

Billy discussed the Johnsons with Duane. "Do they have an account with you?"

"Yes," said Duane, "they generally run a balance. His ranch doesn't do well. He hasn't been able to build much of a herd. They grow some of their food."

"They are sick up there," Billy said as he dried his hands. "The whole family seems to be in poor health. Charlee, Seesoff, and I are going up to work with them tomorrow. I would like to buy a month's worth of supplies in case food is a problem for them."

"Billy, your account has about ten thousand in it. Your house will cost nine or ten thousand. You may want to move a few thousand from your account in Prescott. You have about thirty thousand there."

"I will write a request for withdrawal. The coach from

Prescott will carry it to Verde. I'll hire couriers to bring it from Verde to here. I'll transfer ten thousand." Billy went over to the coffee pot. "Where are Mom's sweet rolls?"

Duane said, "She hasn't brought them over yet. Star is in the storeroom working. I'll have her go over and get some."

Star came out of the storeroom when Duane called. When she saw Billy she ran, jumped up, and gave him a kiss on the cheek. "Hello, Billy. Where have you been?"

"Out hunting and mining. Can't you tell?"

She smiled, "You are a little dirty and smell bad."

Duane asked Star to go over and get some sweet rolls. Without comment, Star headed briskly to the kitchen. She met Mildred. "I need some sweet rolls, Mom."

Mildred smiled, "Hello, Star, how are you? You look nice."

"I'm well, thank you. I try to look nice because I want people to like me."

"When they get to know you they will like you. People just need a little time. We sure think highly of you. You're a good worker. I have noticed more young men customers are coming in, too." Mildred winked.

Star walked lightly back to the store with a full plate of sweet rolls. She put them by the coffee pot and went to straighten some pants on the shelf. Two young men came in and hovered, looking Star over. One stopped close to her and said, "You're a real honey." Star moved to another counter. The man followed and began to obstruct her movements. He kept saying things to her and Star kept moving away.

Finally Duane went over to the two men and said, "I don't know you two boys. Are you from around here?"

"Yeah, we just signed on at the Justin ranch. We're here to get some things."

"Do you have a list? I will help you."

"What about this little darling helping us?" said one of the men. He was a large man, healed with a cross-draw holster and Colt. The other man was smaller and carried a Colt strapped on low.

Duane said, "This girl doesn't wait on customers yet. She is learning and just stocks and cleans. May I help you?"

The smaller man squared off facing Duane. The other man stepped off to the side. The small man said, "We don't want any trouble but we want her to help us."

"Give me your list or leave." The two men were reluctant and stood firm. "Boys, you will be in trouble in three ways if you don't behave. First, Mike Justin will not be happy you caused trouble in this settlement. Two, I'm the justice of the peace and can throw you in jail. Three, that person over there is the acting constable who can arrest you for disturbing the peace. What will it be, boys? Give me the list or leave."

The men looked at each other and gave Duane the list. "Thank you, boys. I'll have it ready in a short time."

Billy wandered over to the men and said, "This girl is only sixteen years old and not ready for advances from men. You were disrespectful by following her around and interfering with her work."

"She's just an Indian," said the larger man. "Age doesn't count for them."

Billy said, "You need to change your attitude about Indians around here. She is very nice and well respected. She is my sister."

"How can that be?" the smaller man said. "You don't look Indian."

Billy patiently explained the relationship. "I hope the next time you're in the settlement you will conduct yourself better."

Duane returned with a large box of merchandise. "Here

you are, boys. You want this on Mike's account or do you wish to pay?"

"Put it on the account," one man said. "You guys throw your weight around for being in such a small settlement. Aren't you short of muscle here?"

"We have a plan for problems. Together we have enough muscle."

"Meaning you and that other fellow is your muscle? What if we wanted to take issue with you and draw down? You are not carrying, and you have just one gun ready."

Duane said, "You wouldn't clear your holster. That man is Billy True."

The men turned pale and stammered, "Do you mean the gunfighter?"

"Yes, do you think that's enough muscle?" The men nodded and left without a word.

Billy said, "That's a good point, Dad. You should wear a gun all the time. You having a gun might prevent a yahoo from drawing."

"You're probably right. I'll start wearing one."

Star came over with a somber look on her face. "That was scary. Did I cause all of that? Did I do something wrong?"

"No," Billy said. "They caused the problem, not you. You're just so darned pretty and bright, I don't know if the world is ready for you." He smiled and gave her a warm hug. Star giggled and returned to her work.

The next morning, Billy, Seesoff, and Charlee loaded the spring wagon. They tied Billy's horse on a lead and started for the Johnson ranch. The ranch lay four miles southeast of the settlement.

The trip took them through a stand of sycamore trees, with their white bark and picturesque branches. They turned up a rutty road for about one mile and approached the ranch from atop a small rise.

The ranch looked unkempt. The corrals were functional but in need of repair. The house and outbuildings were in need of paint. A few cattle grazed in a nearby pasture. Some horses were in a corral adjacent to the barn. A small creek bubbled down past the house and emptied into a little lake.

Elisabeth Johnson greeted them as they came up in front of the house. A young boy clung to his mother's leg as the wagon drew to a stop. Billy tied off the horse at a rail on the side of the house.

"Hello, Elisabeth," Charlee said. "How is your toe?"

"It's much better. You really helped me."

Charlee followed Elisabeth into the house. It was dark and dingy.

"My daughter, Ann, is in the next room," Elisabeth said.

The room was cluttered. An old blanket hung across the one window, blocking the sunlight. Charlee entered and went to the bed. "Ann, my name is Charlee. I have an interesting lady with me. She is an Apache woman called Seesoff. We are here to help you and your family."

Ann said weakly, "Hello, I haven't seen an Indian up close. She is very pretty."

"Thank you," Seesoff said as she moved around the bed and uncovered and opened the window. Air and light poured in.

Ann said, "Mom doesn't want the window open because a draft of air might hurt me."

Charlee went to Elisabeth and said, "She needs more light and air. This will help her health and spirit. You all need more air and light." She returned to the girl. "Ann, can you sit up?" The girl shook her head. Charlee stepped forward, "Let's see what you can do. I'll help you."

Ann struggled and began to cry. "I can't, I can't," the girl whimpered.

Seesoff said, "I will help you." She put her arms around Ann and set her up. Seesoff rubbed Ann's back and shoulders as she held her. This helped the stiffness and pain resulting from inactivity.

"How old are you, Ann?" Charlee asked.

"Seven."

"Look out the window, Ann," said Charlee, "What do you see?"

"I see flowers, trees, and some birds."

"Would you like to go out on the porch and get a closer look?"

Ann pulled up the blankets. "I don't think I can do it, I'm too weak."

"We will help you," Seesoff said.

They rotated Ann off the bed and put her feet on the floor. Ann's legs buckled. "I can't do it," Ann cried.

"Yes, you can," Charlee said softly. Seesoff and Charlee put Ann's arms over their shoulders, walked with her out to the porch, and put her in a chair.

"Here you are, Ann, in a chair on the porch," Seesoff said. "Isn't it nice?"

Ann's five-year-old brother shouted, "Mom, Ann's sitting on the porch in a chair."

Elisabeth, with tears in her eyes, said, "Yes, isn't that nice?"

Seesoff continued to rub Ann's legs, arms, and back to help stiffness and pain.

Ann began to cry, "This is nice."

Charlee said, "Ann, will you let me examine you?"

"Will it hurt?" cried Ann.

"No, honey," Charlee took a tongue blade and examined Ann's teeth and mouth. With the stethoscope Charlee listened to Ann's heart, lungs, and abdomen. "Elisabeth, would you stay here with Ann?"

Charlee walked out to talk to Billy. "Billy, will you take this tube and get some water from the stream where the intake pipe is? If the water turns a brown color, there is contamination. Look at their latrine to see if it's too full. Find out if they had a garden and what they have in the root cellar for food. Thank you."

"Seesoff," Charlee said, "it looks like we have a case of scurvy. Ann's gums are bleeding, and some teeth are loose. The whole family probably has stages of scurvy. We find scurvy in places where diet is limited. The mining camps have a high number of cases. We need to find out what the Johnsons are eating."

Charlee walked to the porch to see how Ann was doing. "How is Ann, Elisabeth?

"She looks better already," Elisabeth said gleefully. "What is the matter with her, Charlee?"

"I think your family has scurvy."

"What is that? Is it bad? Will she die?"

Charlee left Seesoff with Ann and walked with Elisabeth out in the yard. "This could be serious if we don't treat it. Scurvy is caused by a lack of fruit and vegetables in the diet. We think there is some element in these foods that the body needs or you get sick. The sailors on ships used to die of scurvy. It was found that limes and lemons prevented and cured it. That's why English sailors are sometimes called 'Limies.' "

Charlee walked Ann back into the house. "Elisabeth, I

want you to get more fresh air in the house. Ann needs exercise. Take her out on the porch three times a day. This is good for her physically and mentally. Walk to and from her commode and out to the latrine as soon as she is able. You need to clean her up. You need to clean up the whole house. It is important that the whole family bathes and keeps the house clean. Bacteria find a home in dirt. We are going to help you clean some today. We will use soap, water, and carbolic acid on the walls and floors."

Billy checked the water and it was clean. The latrine was full and needed to be moved to another pit. He went to Calvin Johnson to talk to him about the ranch. "Calvin, how many head are you running?"

Calvin said, "Why does a gunfighter want to know about ranching?"

"Mr. Johnson, I'm a rancher too. I'm interested in how you're doing."

"Well, things aren't good. I haven't had a good calving season. My herd is down and I can't afford the services of a good bull."

Billy said, "Would you consider taking in a partner? We can plan how to improve your herd. We can split the profits and build your herd."

"Why should you want to do that?"

"I would like to help out, but I expect to make a profit. I will pay off your account at the store and set up a line of credit."

Calvin said, "My whole family has been sick and I have not been able to keep up with the work. I don't know if I'm a good investment."

Billy moved to sit on a rail. This man was proud and he was hurt by his circumstances. Billy had to be careful how he approached him. "I know what you're saying, but I'm willing to take a chance."

"I don't want to accept charity." Calvin was clearly anguishing over his plight.

Billy said, "A man with a problem is unfortunate, a man who doesn't accept help from neighbors is foolish."

Calvin was silent, clearly thinking on the words from this young scout. "I guess you have a point. I will accept your proposition."

Billy was clearly pleased, smiled, and shook hands with Calvin. "This handshake is an agreement. My word is an ethical contract. I will write up a contract for you to study and sign. I would like to bring a crew up to clean, repair, and paint your place. You will have to accept Indians. I will be with them to supervise. They are good workers."

Calvin pondered the thought of Indians on his place. "It would sure be new to see Indians helping rather than sneaking around to steal or hurt people."

Billy said, "Things are changing, Calvin. We need to change, too. There are good and bad among the Indians. After 1873 the Indians have been mostly peaceful. We fight with the bad Indians but should have more respect for the good."

Billy returned to the house and found Seesoff and Charlee scrubbing and cleaning walls, floors, and furniture. Charlee stopped and walked outside with Billy.

"What did you find out, Billy?"

"The root cellar is practically empty. There are a few old potatoes. I didn't see that they had put up any food in jars. The latrine is full and needs moving. The water seems clean." He told Charlee about his agreement with Calvin.

Charlee said, "That was nice," and gave Billy a kiss and

hug. "Billy, the family is sick with scurvy. They need a lot of fruit and vegetables. They must live better or some of them may die."

This alarmed Billy. "What do we do, Charlee? I brought a box of food but I don't know about fruit and vegetables. I'll bring in the box and we can see what we have."

Charlee returned to the house. Elisabeth was tending Ann. Charlee said, "I want to give Ann a warm bath in your tub. She needs to be thoroughly cleaned and her bedding changed. Seesoff stripped the bed and put on clean linens. Elisabeth, would you mind if we bathed Ann? I want you to drink something and rest a while." Elisabeth was clearly tired from the work. Charlee asked Ann if they could give her a bath while Elisabeth rested.

"It's okay," Ann said. "But I'm a little shy."

Charlee smiled. They prepared a warm, soapy bath in the round washtub. They helped Ann undress and get in the tub. The women washed her hands, legs, and feet thoroughly. Ann enjoyed soaking. They washed her hair with some fragrant shampoo.

Ann was dressed and tucked into bed; she was tired from the activity. Charlee said, "Elisabeth, you need to do this bathing every two or three days. Wash her hands and face daily. The rest of the family should do the same."

Ann piped up, "Miss Charlee, could I meet the gunfighter Mom told me about?" Charlee smiled and went to the door and called Billy in. He came in and walked into the room where Ann was. "Billy, this is Ann and her little brother, Harold."

Billy patted the boy's head and leaned over and kissed Ann on the cheek. The boy stared at Billy's gun. Billy took the boy's hand and rubbed it over the butt of his Colt. Both children were wide-eyed from meeting a bigger-than-life legend. He smiled, said good-bye, and went out to the wagon. He was a little choked up from meeting this little girl and boy.

Seesoff, Charlee, and Billy finished their work and packed up to leave. In the food they had brought were canned fruit, fresh potatoes, and other staples. Charlee said, "We are going home now. We will order some canned foods for you. The food won't be in for a while. We will talk to neighbors about giving us vegetables and fruit. We will be back in two days to check up on your family.

Elisabeth said, "Charlee, I don't know when we will be able to pay you. I appreciate your help."

Charlee said, "Everything will be fine. Make sure you follow my directions."

They headed toward the settlement with their hearts glad.

# Chapter 14: The Raid on the Settlement

Billy was feeling stronger and had been scouting the area around the settlement. He came upon some shod horse tracks up the hill on the north side. It could have been a hunter or a passerby, but it was not a good place to hunt and a hard place to ride for a traveler. He noticed the rider would stop, get off his horse, and stand at a viewpoint of the settlement. The tracks were made at different times. It could be that someone was watching the settlement for some reason.

When Billy returned to the settlement he told Duane about what he had found. Duane was concerned as to why someone would study the settlement.

"Have the warning bells come in?" Billy asked.

"They should be in any day. We'll hang them in Pike's, Bruce's, and the store."

The plan was when someone noticed trouble, people in these sites would pull the wire attached to a bell. The bells would be hung high upon the building in a protected area. The bell would sound the alarm for the settlement.

It was good that preparation was made at the settlement. Danger was lurking. In a small canyon to the west of the settlement, a group of seven men camped. They were there to raid and loot the settlement. They had been watching to see when the least number of people were there. They also watched to see when Billy left and for how long. They determined when Billy left he was usually gone at least three hours. That would give them enough time to complete the raid.

Their plan was to have three riders go in and attack the store, two would cover Pike's, and two would take the blacksmith's shop. They were after cash. They would not bother the women or destroy property. They needed to get in and out fast. The attack would be one hour after the scout left. The gang would have to be prepared to attack every day until Billy left.

On a cloud-covered day, Billy left to visit the Indian camp. He planned to get a hunt in if he had time. Within an hour he was in the camp talking to the leader.

The people in the settlement were busy with their work. Three men rode up to the store and tied off their horses. Star was in the storeroom working. Duane was in front. One man entered and looked around. The two other men came in and locked the door. Duane noticed there was a problem and called to Star and Mildred to stay where they were. The men pulled their guns and demanded the money. Duane said "There is no need for violence if all you want is money."

One man shoved Duane toward the cash drawer. "No talk, just give us the money. Where is your safe?"

Duane said, "All the money we have in the store is in the register."

The man cleaned out the register. "Where is your safe? We

know you have one."

Duane held his hands palm up. "It isn't here."

The man was furious. He hit Duane in the head with his gun. Duane staggered and fell on his back. Star was watching from the storeroom. She went to the wire and rang the bell. Mildred came from the hotel with her Winchester. Star got a Colt from the storeroom. Mildred, peeking from behind a door said, "Leave or we will start shooting."

The men were startled. They had no one to shoot at. Duane was on the floor, without a gun. Another person pushed a Colt through the door to the storeroom. The men dropped down behind some counters, not knowing what to do.

The bell alerted the people at Pike's. Pike locked his door. Two men from the gang were walking toward the saloon. George and his family had also heard the bell and retreated to their firing ports. Charlee and Seesoff heard the bell and decided to stay in the clinic. They had their guns and could push furniture to their window for protection. There was a stalemate.

Duane was coming out of his daze. Assessing the situation, he said, "There has been no real harm done. If you back off now, there will be no shooting. Drop the money and leave."

The men at the store did not know what was happening to the other gang members. The men at the blacksmith's shop found no one there. They had a view of much of the settlement but could see nothing to shoot.

The two men at Pike's couldn't see inside. They started kicking the door. Pike fired a shot from his station. The men outside Pike's started firing blindly at the door and window. That drew fire from Liz and Molly, who were poised at their stations. The men found themselves in a hotbed of gunfire.

They retreated to the side of the saloon near the recreation hall.

Charlee had a view of Pike's from the clinic and fired a warning shot at the men. They dropped to their bellies and crawled into the recreation center.

The men at the blacksmith shop started toward the saloon. Shots from George's place pinned them down.

At Murphy's, the men had heard shots from other places and wondered what was happening. One tried to work toward the door, but Mildred fired a round near him. One of the intruders shouted at Duane, "You on the floor, stop this shooting or I will shoot you."

Duane said, "You fellows need to understand you're under many guns. If you let me, I'll try to calm everyone down and get you out without getting people killed."

One man said, "I want to talk to the other men."

Duane said, "We will go together." He got a white rag and tied it to a mop handle. As they opened the door to go out Duane shouted, "Hold your fire, we're coming out!" To the man, he added, "You had better holster your gun."

The man put his gun away. They walked to the center of the street. The man went to talk to his men. He came back and said, "If you give us a thousand dollars we will leave."

Duane said, "I should point out you are in a crossfire trying to get out of town. You will leave empty-handed or die here."

The man went back to his men and discussed the situation. He came back to Duane and said they would leave. The men went to their horses, mounted, and collected in the street.

Duane told them, "We are well armed and trained."

The leader said, "We really don't know that, do we?"

Duane said, "Don't come back here again or we will shoot

you. Pass the word that this settlement is no place to mess around."

The gang moved out wondering what would have happened if they had continued the raid.

Duane went around congratulating everyone. They all came out into the street to praise and talk to each other. Star and Molly were crying from the stress of the incident.

Charlee said, "We just had a brush from the danger of this territory. There was no gunfire at us. Luck was on our side. This was scary for us. I guess this gives us an idea about some of the things Billy has gone through."

Duane came out of the store with a bandage on his head. "I'm proud of you all. We successfully tested our defense system. We were all ready and at our stations. Thanks go to Star, who rang the bell alerting you."

Charlee went over to look at Duane's head. "You will need a couple of stitches. Come over and I will treat the wound." They headed over to the clinic. "Where is Ring?" Charlee asked. "Have you seen him?"

They went to the store and called for Ring. They went into the café and hotel, looking and calling his name. Charlee finally found Ring hiding under a staircase quivering from fright. "Come here, Ring," Charlee said gently. Ring came over and buried his head into her hands and whimpered. Charlee patted and rubbed his ears. "All the gunfire must have scared him," she said. "Let's take him with us over to the clinic where it's quiet." Charlee treated Duane's head with two small sutures.

A few hours later, things had settled down and people were at their work. It was fortunate that ranchers and their families were not in town when the raid happened.

Billy rode into the settlement and went to see Charlee. She

explained what had happened. He gave her a kiss and went over to the store to see Duane.

"Hi," Duane said as Billy entered the store. "You missed a little excitement."

"Did you get any licks in?"

"No," said Duane. "We were able to negotiate our way out of trouble."

"Dad, this doesn't feel right. These guys plan and carry out attacks. They take their booty and disappear to show up in another area when their money runs out. They are in trouble when they can't buy provisions."

"What are you saying, Billy? Will they come back?" Duane held a hand to his head.

"I think there is a strong possibility they will come back. They need money. They will have to leave the area soon to keep a posse or the army from getting them. They won't come tonight because they are at a disadvantage in the dark. If they come, it will be early tomorrow morning and try to catch us asleep."

"Our people will be frightened," Duane said as he adjusted the bandage on his head. "I don't know how ready we can get them."

Billy, with a great deal of concern, said, "We will get into our stations tonight and be waiting at daybreak. I'll go around and talk to everyone. They need to understand we won't shoot to warn them. They will attack and try to break down doors to get inside. We need to keep them in the street and shoot them."

Billy went around to the people to give them instructions. He was surprised to find them relatively calm. They started to get food, water, and blankets to their stations. He went to tell Charlee and Seesoff to go to the store. That would put more guns at the point of the greatest threat. He would be at Pike's to help there. George's place was ready to keep the gang from taking cover in the corrals.

Billy went to nail shut the doors and windows of the recreation center, jail, and the clinic. This would keep the gang from taking cover there.

At sunrise the gang hit the settlement in three places. Four men attacked the store, two hit the saloon, and one was at the corrals. Gunfire erupted from all stations. The gang fired wildly at the doors and windows. At first they could not find where the shooting was coming from. The men left their horses and tried to enter the buildings. They were met with shots from several directions.

The man at the corrals went down immediately with shots from George's stations. The four men at the store tried to circle around behind the building but were met with gunfire. The gang began firing at the gun ports. These were small targets for them. The two men at Pike's place tried to find cover in the jail and recreation center but could not get in. They went down by vicious fire from the saloon.

The men left were those at the store. They hugged the walls and porch to find cover. The guns from Pike's and George's were turned on the store. Two men were killed and the other two cried for surrender.

Duane told them to drop their guns and walk into the street. He called to the other stations to hold their fire. People emerged from their stations.

Billy shouted, "Be careful! Make sure those men down are dead or helpless."

At Pike's there was a casualty: Molly had been hit from a bullet coming through the gun port. Billy called for Charlee to come quick.

Charlee found Molly on the floor with cuts on her face from wood fragments and a bullet hole in her chest. Charlee said, "I hope that was a spent bullet when it hit her. We have to get her over to the clinic where I can work." Billy picked Molly up and carried her toward the clinic.

Molly cried, "I'm sorry, Billy, I tried hard to shoot and hit something."

Billy said, "You did fine, Molly. We're proud of you."

He placed Molly on a table and Charlee looked at the wound. Blood oozed from Molly's chest and onto the table. Charlee put a compress on the wound and asked Billy to hold it. Charlee went to get her forceps and bullet extractor.

Molly started crying, "It hurts, Charlee. Billy, I'm afraid."

Charlee said, "Billy, hold her hand and put the palm of your other hand on her forehead."

"Charlee," Molly asked, "will people still love me with scars on my face?"

"We will love you no matter what, Molly," Charlee said. "Seesoff, start the chloroform mask."

Charlee tried the forceps first but the bullet was too deep. She tried her bullet extractor and was able to remove the bullet. She told Seesoff to stop the chloroform drip and remove the mask. Molly awoke and said, "It hurts bad, Charlee."

Charlee stroked Molly's forehead and said, "I'm sorry, Molly. I'll give you something for the pain." She gave her some laudanum.

Molly cried and said she was afraid. Seesoff put her face next to Molly's face and whispered, "I have asked my god to heal your wounds." Molly fell off to sleep.

Seesoff and Charlee stayed with Molly through the day. They washed her face and arms with cool water to hold the fever down.

Billy and Duane had taken the two surviving gang members to the jail and locked them up. George and his boys loaded the bodies of the gang on a wagon. They took identification and personal effects to send to Prescott. The bodies were taken to the cemetery for burial.

Everyone was concerned for Molly. No one else had been hurt in the brief fighting. Billy and Duane stood guard during the day. The others went to bed for a rest before the work started.

The next day Charlee came over to the store. Mildred and Duane greeted her with a cup of coffee and a hug. Charlee started crying. "Molly is dead. The bullet caused internal bleeding and maybe some damage to organs. I couldn't do anything to save her. I don't know enough."

Mildred said, "You did all you could, Charlee. That's all anyone could ask."

"That's not good enough for me," Charlee said. "I need to learn more." She sat down to rest and reflect on her memory of Molly. Ring came up and crawled on her lap. They both needed some comfort.

The settlement took Molly's death hard. Everything considered, they realized things could have been worse and that their plan for defense was good. Duane was preparing a report to send to Prescott about the raid. Billy was going around checking and cleaning the guns. People coming into the settlement were amazed by what had happened.

Billy went over to see Charlee and talk to her about Molly. The people who knew her would miss her smiling face and humor. They sat together on the porch swing and talked about the defense of the settlement. Billy said, "We don't have time to get help into the settlement. If the gang had hit us the same way the first time, I don't know if we could have held. We may have to hire security to be on guard all the time."

Charlee said, "Billy, I don't know if I can do this. I don't have a lot of help. I'm isolated here with heavy responsibility. People will depend on me to diagnose and treat their problems, but I don't know if I'm strong or courageous enough."

Billy said, "If you're not strong or courageous enough, I don't know who is. I love you because you are those things and a lot more. You're all we have. Just like me, people rely on my guns to protect them. I don't know if I'll always be up to it."

Charlee said with a smile, "If you're not up to it, who is?" She rested her head on his shoulder and he rested his chin on the crown of her head.

# Chapter 15: Troop Recognition in Verde

Billy had recovered well and was exercising with his weights at the store. His weights were poured cement in various sizes of cans, with iron bars connecting them. Billy ran in the hills around the settlement. He also spent several hours a week shooting his guns, drawing and firing for accuracy. Charlee often joined in the shooting and strength training with Billy.

They had acquired land one mile north of the settlement. It abutted open range to the east and was a combination of mining claims, land grants, and homestead. The couple had contracted with Duane to acquire the materials for a house, which was to be large with plenty of room for a family. Plans were obtained from a catalogue, and Charlee was liberal in her modification of the plans.

Charlee opened her health clinic in Dr. Pierce's house when he left. Dr. Pierce decided to buy new equipment so that he wouldn't have to move everything in his office. This meant that Charlee was able to buy the old equipment and stocks of medications. The date for the wedding had not been set. Bertha was working on the wedding plans with some help from Mildred. She seemed happy to help out. Her relationship with Billy was warming.

A letter arrived from General Crook asking Billy and the family to attend a special ceremony in Verde. The ceremony was to recognize the cavalry detachment that destroyed Rudd Leland. A Presidential Unit Citation was to be given to the troop, with Billy included. Billy was pleased to go if the recognition was going to the troops. He had a high regard for the fighting Tenth Cavalry.

The ceremony would be the next month—September 15. The family seemed pleased to take a little vacation together. Duane and Mildred, the Darrows, Seesoff, and Star would go. They would need two large spring wagons. Billy and two Arrow hands would be on horseback for escort. They would take two extra horses along in case one went lame. The group would take two and a half days to reach Verde. This would require camping and security measures.

Seesoff and Star concerned Charlee. She had talked to Billy about their standard of living. They had decided to talk to Duane about bringing them into the settlement to live. Duane, however, was concerned about the reaction from the other inhabitants and ranchers.

"I think you're right about their welfare," Duane said. "We need to discuss it with George, Pike, and some of the ranchers."

Billy said, "It would be well to get their feelings, but they don't have a veto over our decisions."

Duane agreed, "That's true, but the ladies should try to modify their dress and ways to adapt to the White world."

Charlee said, "We can talk to them and work to make the necessary changes. They are very lovely women. Dress them up and they will knock your eyes out. Particularly little Star."

Billy said, "They can live in Pierce's house. Dad, you own the house, I could buy it from you. The women are my responsibility. I gave my word to Buckskin Hat that I would take care of them. I intend to do what's best for them. If anyone harms or mistreats them, they will answer to me. The community needs to understand my responsibility to these women. Charlee and I love them very much."

Duane said, "Billy, it would be well if I talk to those people. People fear and respect you, and might hold back their feelings."

Billy responded, "You have a good point. I hate to think I will spend my life with people being afraid of me. I guess my guns have spoken too loudly in the past."

Billy and Charlee were concerned about the women's feelings about leaving some of their culture to adapt to the White world.

"Charlee, I think we should take Seesoff and Star on a horseback ride up into the mountains for a talk. The spirits of nature will help us clear our thoughts, and the women can make their feelings heard."

Charlee responded thoughtfully, "That would be a good thing. We have been making plans for them without knowing for sure how they feel."

"I will talk to them about the ride," Billy said. Charlee and Billy left to talk to Mildred in the kitchen.

"Mom," Charlee said, "Would it be possible for Billy and me to live in the hotel until our house is finished? We will need separate rooms and we will pay rent."

Mildred said, "I think that would work. How long will the house take?"

"We have hired a contractor to build the house. He's

bringing a crew but has agreed to use Indian labor when possible."

Billy interrupted Charlee to say, "Dad is ordering the materials now. This should speed up the job. I will pay the contractor in four stages, depending on his progress. This process should keep things moving along. Once the material is in and they start, it should be done before the Ghost Face of winter arrives."

Billy looked at Charlee and said, "I'm sorry to interrupt you," and kissed her lightly on the lips.

"That's okay, White Warrior," Charlee said with a smile.

They had arranged for Seesoff and Star to join them on a ride and a picnic on a nearby mountain mesa. The women were happy for a break in their work and to get out on a nice ride. The group left midmorning of the next day. Mildred had prepared a hefty lunch and packed it into Billy's pommel bags. Billy and Charlee were armed with Colts and Winchesters, while Seesoff and Star had Winchesters in their saddle scabbards.

Their trail took them through madrone trees with their red bark, and there were chokeberry trees around the springs. Black-tailed jacks and cottontails scurried through the bushes. Quail called out as the troop entered some scattered ponderosa pine and honey mesquite. The trip was pleasant and conducive to easy conversation about the wonders of nature.

The mountain mesa opened up into a plethora of wild flowers and budding trees. They stopped at a place with scattered shade and pine needles for their blankets to lie on. The horses were hobbled to graze nearby while Billy looked over the area with his glass.

"The world is nice here," Billy commented as he noticed

some deer grazing in a meadow at the end of the mesa. "I've spent many hours here listening to the sounds of nature and getting close to the spirit world."

They enjoyed their lunch of beef sandwiches, boiled eggs, and coffee. They moved to lie on the blankets to watch the billowing clouds make shapes. It was very serene and everyone enjoyed the peacefulness of the day.

Billy rose to study the source of a whistling sound. He smiled, "That sound is made by the wind blowing through a dry acorn on an oak tree down below. Indians sometimes try to make the sound to signal, but this is real."

Naps were in order for the women as the day dwindled into the afternoon. Billy, always the scout, perused the borders of the mesa. Things were well as he watched a deer wander into a little meadow. The thoughts of the day drifted into his focus.

"Ladies, we need to start thinking about going home." The women roused themselves, and Charlee jumped on Billy in a playful scuffle.

Righting herself from her play, Charlee asked, "Are you ladies happy working in the settlement?"

"I'm very happy," sounded Star with a smiling face.

Seesoff, with a questioning look, added, "I find the settlement and people very challenging and exciting. Is there a problem, Charlee?"

Charlee appreciated an opportunity to make a point. "We have wondered if you ladies would like to move to the settlement and live at the Pierce house. I know this would be a major change, but we thought it would mean a better future for you."

Star asked, "Would this mean we would not be Indians if we live more in the White world?"

Seesoff spoke strongly, "We will always be Indians, Star. Our world might change, but we will take the values of out culture with us."

"We respect the Indian culture," Billy said, "but we believe the White man's world will overcome the Indian culture. Things will not be much better for Indians. We want you to consider living in and enjoying the benefits of the White world. You could keep the values of Indian culture."

Seesoff stepped forward to capture the others' attention. "We have lived on reservations for years. Life is hard and the old ways are lost in the changes we are forced to make. I wish more for myself and Star, but I want to be encouraged to keep my heritage in mind. What do you think, Star?"

With her eyes lifted to gaze directly at Billy, Star replied, "I will do what my brother wishes—he always helps me and wants the best for us. I want a better life, with education, and to live in a better new world. I see these things in the settlement among the Whites. Is it wrong for me to think like this?"

Seesoff hugged Star, saying, "No, it's not bad, but always remember your Indian culture."

Billy, speaking with compassion and authority, said, "I think Buckskin Hat would approve your seeking a better life and at the same time remembering your roots."

Charlee spoke cautiously, "Do you want to move into the settlement and live more in the White world?"

Seesoff and Star, looking at each other with a pause, agreed they would make this life-changing move.

The group freed their horses from the hobble, saddled them, and prepared to leave. The mood was somber as each person thought of what was about to happen in their lives. On the ride back, the serenity and beauty of nature encouraged them—life would be better. They arrived at the settlement at dusk.

Readying for the trip to Verde dominated the family's time. The Murphys' store would be closed while they were gone. George would watch over the place and open the store if people needed things. Charlee was spending more time at the ranch. She also was working with Seesoff and Star on a new wardrobe. They had agreed with the need to change behavior and dress. It was Charlee's charge to get the women ready to go to Verde.

Billy was working with George to get the spring wagons ready for the trip. Duane was working on getting the house started. Bertha was working happily on the wedding. Mildred was developing menus and clothing for the trip. All seemed well.

The group was well armed, with excellent provisions. Billy was on the point, scouting ahead and circling the flanks. He stopped periodically to scan the country with his glass. They stopped to camp after a long day. Billy posted the riders around the camp. After dinner he set up his station on the side of a hill for defensive purposes. The group rested well during the night.

The next morning Billy was up and had scouted the area before waking the others. "Get up, everyone. The stream is nice and fresh to wash up. The coffee is on. I have scouted the area and things look good. We are at the west end of the rim. It will be a little rough until we clear the higher mountains. We have good rigs and strong horses, though, so it shouldn't be too bad."

The group had a good breakfast and Billy relieved the riders from lookout duty. He perched up the hill fifty yards to view the road and surrounding hills. Charlee came up to sit with him. Billy worked his glass down the road and up the flanks. The area was clear and serene. "We are getting closer to the fort. Intruders won't work this close to the army. We should be in Verde early the day after tomorrow. We will put up in the guest quarters and wait for the ceremony the next day."

The next day the going was harder but the group, horses, and equipment held up well. They were over the high mountains and camped for the night. They followed the routine from the night before. Billy did his scouting and posted the guards. He climbed to a vantage point to set his station for the night. Charlee climbed up to sit with him. They caressed as they said good night. Charlee climbed down to the camp and said good night to the others and went to bed.

Early the next morning Charlee awoke to the horses acting up and sounding off. She grabbed her Colt and was within thirty yards of the string when she saw a large mountain lion on a rock above the stock. She pulled up her Colt in a two-hand hold and fired two rounds. The cat jumped and fell down beside the rock. Billy came running down with his Winchester ready.

Coming upon the scene, Billy said with clear admiration in his voice, "That was a great shot, Charlee. You hit him in the side with both rounds. That's a great grouping—it's as good as anybody could shoot. I'm proud of you."

Charlee flushed and said, "Thank you. I guess our practice paid off."

Billy took the cat by the tail and dragged it thirty yards away. "I'm going to bury it to keep the scent from bothering the horses." The rest of the group came to see the cat. Charlee showed them where she was standing when she made the shot.

Willard said, "That's a great shot with a hand gun. Charlee, you can stand tall with anyone in your shooting, even Billy."

Charlee responded, "Not really. It's one thing to shoot and not be hit. It's another when you're fighting. No one matches my warrior in combat."

Billy smiled, "You might be surprised with yourself if the time should come. Always be ready to shoot if needed; don't hesitate."

After the cat was buried, Billy checked the horses. He gave them some grain to help calm them down and asked Charlee to rub their noses and talk to them. He put the shovel away and washed his hands with strong soap to kill the cat scent. Then he gave Charlee a kiss on the lips and whispered warm things to her.

As Billy saddled his horse he said, "Let's get some breakfast going. I'm going to look around." He rode zigzag patterns in the hills around the camp. When he came back there was a healthy breakfast waiting for him. The others were packing up to travel.

"The way looks clear. You riders take the flanks, I'll ride the point." Billy spurred and rode down the road.

They were in sight of Fort Verde early in the afternoon. The group was relieved to be near their destination. Billy rode ahead and was challenged at the gate by a guard. "I am Billy True and this is my party to attend the ceremony tomorrow."

"Yes, sir," said the guard as he snapped to attention and presented his rifle in salute. Billy saluted back as a courtesy. They proceeded on to the administration building near the southeast corner of the compound. On the left was the parade ground where the ceremony would be held. The wagons stopped in front and Billy dismounted and went into the administration office.

A captain received him cordially and the group was directed to the bachelor officers' quarters. They parked the wagons behind the quarters and placed the horses in the cavalry corral. The men would have to bunk in the company quarters across the parade ground from the bachelor officers' quarters, while the ladies would stay in the officers' quarters.

A problem developed when Seesoff and Star entered the compound. A young lieutenant stopped Billy and said Indians were not allowed on the fort grounds.

Billy said, "If they don't come in, neither do the rest of us. Call your officer of the day, please."

The lieutenant left and returned with a captain from the administrative office. "Sir," he said, "it is against regulations to have Indians on the post without special approval."

Billy said, "This is my Indian mother and sister. If they don't come in, I'm leaving with the rest of my family. This territory has to start accepting Indians as citizens if we are to have tranquility. If you need to get approval from General Crook for them to pass, I expect this to be done immediately so as not to embarrass my family."

The officer saluted Billy and returned to the administrative office. A few minutes later the captain returned and said, "General Crook said you are to pass but have responsibility for the members of your party."

"Thank you," said Billy as he mounted and led the way to the bachelor officers' quarters. The ladies were situated in the quarters and seemed pleased with the attention given them.

Billy was escorted to the commanding officer's quarters where he met General Crook. The general was very cordial and interested in the recent action against Leland. The general was particularly interested in Billy's Colt.

Crook said, "According to the troops, your Colts spewed

out lightning bolts and terrorized the enemy. What say you, Scout?"

"Just .44/40 slugs, sir."

The General said, "Your Colts are a treasure for our military history. I would like to have them to display with the story of your exploits in the Leland battle."

Billy said, "If you want them, they are yours. I don't know about displaying them."

Crook smiled, "The territory needs examples of our soldiers' bravery. This is a good example."

"I have been planning to buy some black Colts that wouldn't reflect light. You may have mine and I will order the new ones."

"I have a friend in the Colt Company. Let me order you some custom Colts at their expense. It would be an honor for me and them."

Billy held out his hand to shake the general's. "I would welcome that trade. You will have my Colts when I leave tomorrow."

Billy discussed his pride in the troops that fought with him in the battle.

Crook said, "I understand the battle plan was yours."

"I had help from Lieutenant Evans and Sergeant Hooks," Billy insisted.

General Crook, seeking an advantage, said, "Can I persuade you to join the regular army as an officer and chief of the scouts?"

"I'm sorry, sir. I'm getting married and my future wife has other plans for me."

"Ahh, and who is this influential lady?"

"Charlee Rae Darrow, a very special woman."

"I have heard of her. From the reports she is a magnificent

woman." The general clapped Billy on the back. "Well done, son," he grinned.

The meeting broke up and they left to prepare for dinner in the officers' mess. At the dinner they met Mark Evans, who was there to participate in the ceremony. Charlee said hello and extended her hand to Mark. Mark took it and held it for a moment. Then he gently lowered his hand, looked at Charlee a final time, and turned to Billy.

"Billy True," he said and shook Billy's hand. "How are you?"

"Fine, thank you," Billy said. He nodded his head, took Charlee's arm, and moved on.

After dinner they went to the ladies' quarters to socialize. Charlee talked about her training in Prescott and the plans for the new house.

The party broke up, Mark left, and Billy stayed to be with Charlee. The day had been full and all were ready for bed. Charlee held Billy close and told him, "I love you, Billy." Billy nodded and kissed her good night.

The next morning they had breakfast and went to prepare for the ceremony. Chairs were placed near the road in front of the administrative building and faced the parade ground so everyone could see. Troops formed up on the parade ground.

Billy left his quarters and went to visit the members of the special detachment he had fought with. He met Sergeant Hooks and shook his hand vigorously. "Here we meet again under more pleasant circumstances," Billy said.

Hooks smiled in agreement. "Scout, you look well. How is Miss Charlee?"

"She is well and we are to be married soon."

"She is certainly full of spunk. She will give you good sons."

Billy leaned in. "Don't let her hear you say that, Sergeant.

She has been bothering me for some time about having sons. That seems to be the first order of business when we get married."

The sergeant laughed and they went on to say hello to the rest of the detachment. The troop was getting ready for the ceremony. Everything gleamed with polish. The freshly washed horses glowed. Infantry and cavalry troops filled the parade ground. The detachment would be front and center, all eyes upon them.

Billy left to put on his new store suit. He looked quite snappy as he walked across the parade grounds to get Charlee's approval. As he walked past the assembled troops, the officer in charge called the troops to attention. They saluted as Billy walked by. Billy stopped repeatedly to return the salutes as he passed through the ranks.

When he arrived to see Charlee his face was flushed and his voice full of disbelief and joy as he told her what had happened.

Charlee said firmly, "You are a great warrior and are due the respect. Enjoy it."

Billy noticed the ladies in their pressed and fluffy dresses. The older ladies dressed conservatively, the younger with spirit. Charlee, Seesoff, and Star wore colorful prints and draped shawls over their shoulders to ward off the cool breeze.

"What a gathering of charm," Billy said. "It will be a pleasure to escort such a covey of ladies." Charlee gave Billy a look to check his new suit.

"You look nice, too, Billy," Charlee said as she looked him over. "I wonder when we are supposed to go over to the ceremony site?"

"They will send an escort to take us over so we won't

wander around." He noticed Seesoff and Star in their new clothes. "You ladies look beautiful in your new dresses." The women playfully curtsied to Billy. The time had come. The men joined the ladies and awaited direction. Two officers came and asked to escort the party to the parade ground. They were led around the grounds to the rows of chairs located in front of the administrative office. Billy's party was seated in front, facing the podium.

It was impressive. The troops filled the parade ground with the special detachment center-front. Fourteen of them and an empty horse saddled with boots turned backward in the stirrups. This signified a fallen comrade. Mark and Sergeant Hooks led the troop.

A bugle sounded and the troops came to attention. The general and his staff marched to the front and called for the parade to rest. This command told them to be at ease.

General Crook approached the podium and asked the visitors to sit. He went through a litany of courtesies and introduction of officers and guests from government. When all the introductions were made, Crook described the action they were recognizing. He told the story of the battle. He described the courage and effectiveness of the troops and the importance of destroying Rudd Leland's gang.

Clearing his throat and taking some water, the general said, "It is hard not to get emotional when I talk about this detachment of troops. They symbolize the quality of our troops and are appreciated by a grateful country. I have the honor of recognizing some of them for special performance. Would Lieutenant Mark Evans dismount and step forward?" Mark came forward and stood in front of the general. "For meritorious performance under fire, I award you the Certificate of Merit. You are also promoted to captain in rank."

Mark said, "Thank you, sir." He returned and mounted his horse.

The general called out, "Would Sergeant Hooks please dismount and come forward?" Hooks came to the front and stood before the general. "For meritorious performance under fire, and the effort to save the scout by treating his wounds and transporting him to the settlement, I award you the Certificate of Merit. You will also receive an increase in pay of two dollars a month." Hooks thanked him and returned to mount his horse.

The general said, "It is a great honor to award the Presidential Unit Citation to this troop. This is the highest honor a troop can receive. Congratulations." On his command the troop saluted. The general was impressed and pleased. He continued. "The trooper who was killed also receives the same recognition." The general paused for a moment of silence.

He continued, "The people in the settlement gave special treatment to the troops while they were there. The troop had a plaque made to show their appreciation." He looked toward Billy, Star, Seesoff, and Charlee. "I have chosen a person to represent them. This person represents the spirit of this territory and the wave of the future. Would Charlee Rae Darrow come forward please?"

Charlee's mouth fell open in astonishment. "What should I do, Billy?"

"You will have to go up there," Billy said with a grin.

Charlee stood and walked up in front of the general. "This plaque represents the gratitude of the troop to the settlement for the treatment they received." Charlee took the plaque and bowed, then curtsied.

"I understand you are a medicine woman, ranch hand, and

157

an excellent shot with a gun?"

Charlee smiled and said, "Yes, sir, I try."

"My scout said he would not join the regular army because you had other plans for him."

"That's true, General, starting with our marriage and a son."

The troop laughed loudly and was called to order by Mark.

The general excused Charlee to return to her seat. Billy said, "That was nice, Charlee. What if we have a girl?"

"We will love her dearly and then have a son."

General Crook rearranged some papers, cleared his throat, and said, "Would Lieutenant Billy True, Chief Scout, come forward?"

Billy hesitated, rose, and went to the general.

The general spoke. "In front of this assembly I will say I have never heard of a soldier with more courage than this man. He is just twenty years old and is a legend in the territory. Schoolchildren talk of him as a hero. People say his Colts shoot lightning bolts. His charge at Leland's attack column was something never seen or heard of. His courage to rise, after being seriously wounded, mount, and ride over a mile to engage Rudd Leland in hand-to-hand combat was extraordinary. He received another wound in his thigh and lunged with his knife to kill Leland. He cut off Leland's pigtail and sent it to me." The general raised the hair and showed it to the crowd. A gasp went up. The general shook the pigtail. "True says he didn't scalp Leland, but there is a little skin around the edges." The troop laughed again and was called to order.

"Billy True, you are awarded the Presidential Unit Citation along with the troop. I am giving you a lieutenant's commission in the inactive reserve. With the recommendation of your commanding officer, the Congress of the United States, and a special recommendation by the president, I award you the Congressional Medal of Honor."

Stunned, Billy faltered and then caught himself. The general placed the Medal of Honor around his neck. Thunderous applause drowned Billy's thanks.

As Billy walked to his seat, Charlee leaned over to her mother and said, "Is my warrior good enough for me now?"

Bertha shrugged, "Yes."

Billy sat down next to Charlee and whispered, "You're going to have to help me with all of this. I don't know how to deal with it or what to say to people."

"We will deal with it together."

A reception for the guests in the general's quarters followed the awards. Seesoff and Star clung to Billy's arms with Charlee right behind. As they approached the general's quarters Seesoff and Star drifted off and Charlee came alongside Billy.

They were a striking couple and impressed the guests and officers. People seemed to want to touch Billy. They shook his hand, and ladies came close to feel his presence. Charlee stayed extra close to Billy.

Glory bright as sunshine surrounded Billy and Charlee. Lovely, bright, and gracious, Seesoff and Star were also much admired. Raised in fear and separated by culture, many people had never been so close to an Indian. As they talked with Star and Seesoff, the fear in their differences evaporated.

All was well as the evening came to a close.

The next morning the friends and family breakfasted and began packing. Billy took his guns over to General Crook. The general was pleased. He obtained the specifications for the guns he was getting for Billy. They were two Colt Peacemakers, solid black, one with a six-inch barrel and one with an eight-inch barrel. "Billy," the general said, "is this the knife you killed Leland with?"

"Yes," Billy said. "I suppose you want it also?"

"Yes," said the General. "It will be of great interest displayed with your guns."

Billy lifted his knife from its sheath and handed it to the general. "Now I really feel naked without my gun and knife. Dad better have replacements for me when I get to the wagon or I'll be back for these." He saw the general's face and added. "Dad will. Thanks very much, General."

Billy left the headquarters and walked to the barracks where he met Sergeant Hooks. "It has been quite an experience, Sergeant. Can I see the troops?" They walked down the line and Billy shook the hand of each trooper. The troops were pleased and realized that Billy was not just a legend but a comrade in arms.

Billy left the barracks and walked to the parade grounds to see the ladies. He saw Mark talking to Charlee. His breath quickened and his arms stiffened but he caught himself and shrugged it off. Charlee was his, he told himself, and Mark a comrade in arms.

"Hello," said Billy. "How are you folks this morning?" Charlee stepped forward and gave Billy a hug and a kiss. Billy shook Mark's hand.

"Billy, Mark has asked an interesting question you need to answer."

"What is it, Mark?" Billy asked, barely concealing his impatience.

Mark moved nervously. "I was wondering if I could call on Star, if I have an opportunity, in the future."

Billy couldn't hide his surprise. "She is only sixteen and has not become used to our ways. That will take time. You would have difficulty in the army with her. Are you serious? If you hurt her, you answer to me."

"I meant in the future, Billy. My intentions are honorable." The soldier took a breath. "By the way," he added, "I have not seen you without your guns before. Are you any good with your hands?"

Charlee intruded, standing between the men. "Mark," she said, "Billy is deadly with his hands. I have seen him in action. Don't seek an opportunity to test him. We appreciate you asking about Star. Let's leave it there for now."

"Good-bye, Charlee," Mark said and left for his quarters. Charlee soothed Billy, seeing the ire on his face. "Billy, you need to get used to men paying attention to Star and Seesoff. They are standouts in this country of few women."

"Am I going to have to fight all the unwanted suitors of these women?"

"I doubt many would want to face you."

Over the next two days the group made an uneventful trip back to the settlement. Things were well at home. The group went into Murphy's to freshen up. Billy and Charlee retreated to the porch to spend some time alone.

Late summer had arrived and the weather was comfortable. "This is a good time for the wedding," Billy said. "It would be nice if the house was done before what the Indians call 'Ghost Face of Winter' comes."

Charlee nodded and sighed. They were happy, young, and thankful for the challenges and encouragements that life offered. They sat close, impatient with waiting for their marriage.

Duane had talked to many people in the area about Seesoff and Star moving into the settlement. There was some resistance, and feelings toward Indians were still kind of raw, but the people in the settlement approved the move. They'd had the opportunity to come to know the women well. Billy made the decision to move the women into the Pierce house. He and Duane took the spring wagon and moved Seesoff and Star in one morning.

# Chapter 16: Seesoff Finds Romance

When Trae Smith came back to have his leg checked, Charlee removed the drain and stitches. A small wound remained where the drain had been. Trae insisted that Seesoff bandage the leg and Charlee sensed there was more to this visit than his wound. Trae seemed smitten with Seesoff. She moved close to him as she worked. Trae's breathing quickened and his freckled skin flushed deep red.

Before Trae left, he took Charlee aside and asked, "Do you think I could call on Miss Seesoff?" Charlee told him Billy was the guardian of the two Indian women. He had promised their father he would protect them.

Charlee said, "So, Trae, two things have to happen. First, Seesoff has to approve. Secondly, you have to talk to Billy and ask his permission."

Trae said, "I don't think he's man enough to stop me from seeing Seesoff."

"Don't test him," Charlee said as she rolled bandages. "People bigger and younger than you have tried. Just go along and see his side and you will be all right."

Trae smiled at Seesoff as he left the clinic. Seesoff sped over to Charlee's side.

"What did he say, Charlee?"

"Oh, just that he is falling in love and wants to call on you."

"My goodness," Seesoff gasped. "What should I do, Charlee?"

Charlee smiled. "How do you feel, Seesoff?"

"I have warm feelings for Trae. I don't know much about him."

They moved into the front room and sat in the blue padded chairs. Charlee said, "I've known Trae for many years. His wife died ten years ago from influenza. She was a slight and feeble woman. Trae was really good to her. They had no children and he is about forty years old. He might still want children. Are you up to having children, Seesoff?"

"I don't know, Charlee. If he would be a good father, it could be possible. I have not been in love or intimate with anyone. I don't know what to expect in a romantic relationship. I would have to wait and see."

A scratch at the door drew Charlee to open it and she found Ring begging to come in. "Come in, boy. How are you?" She scratched his ears and head. "You rascal, how did you get out of Murphy's? Lie down here." Charlee put Ring next to her chair and continued to rub his head absently.

Charlee adjusted her chair to face Seesoff directly. "We have to be concerned about how Billy will take this. He knows how Trae feels about Indians. It will be hard to sell Billy on the thought that Trae has changed."

Seesoff asked, "Charlee, how much should I listen or respect Billy's wishes? I know he is sincere about his role as my guardian. I was there when he committed himself to Star and me. Yet I'm older than he is!"

"Seesoff, do you want me to talk to Billy to soften him up a little?" Charlee smiled, "I do have some influence with him." They both laughed.

"It might help if you present the issue to Billy. I'm sure he has no idea that Trae feels this way.... Charlee, can Trae support a wife?"

Charlee reflected. "He has a well-kept 500-cow ranch up the hill on the west side of the settlement. He seems to have plenty of everything. He has a nice spring wagon with a brace of strong horses. We could ask Duane about Trae's accounts."

Seesoff nodded. "I guess we will have to wait and see what happens."

Later that evening, Charlee and Billy sat on the hotel porch discussing their wedding date, set for November 15, 1879, just a few weeks away.

The worlds of other people filled their lives. There were many things afoot that needed resolving. Billy had to work with Calvin Johnson on the ranch. The logistics of the wedding needed planning with Bertha and Mildred. The progress on the house needed to be monitored. Billy and the Darrows' relationship had to be improved. Billy wanted to continue placer mining to make up the cost of the house.

"Oh, by the way, Billy," Charlee said as she softened him up with a hug and kiss. "Trae Smith is interested in Seesoff and wants to call on her."

"What? Where in the world did this come from?" Billy sat up straight. "He hates Indians. What are his motives? She is a wonderful person, not a thing to play with."

"I don't think he has bad thoughts, Billy. He may have some serious thoughts about marriage. He is a lonely man."

"What does Seesoff think?" Billy fired. He made a fist and grabbed it with his other hand. Charlee took his hands in hers.

"Billy, Seesoff has warm feelings for him. But, of course, she is concerned about what you might think. You need to be careful with her feelings. Hold your temper. Call on the scout in you to have patience."

"I'll try," Billy fumed. "It depends on how he responds to me, though."

Billy kissed Charlee on her forehead lightly and went to talk with Seesoff.

"Seesoff, what is this relationship with Trae Smith?" His voice was hushed but she knew he was disturbed.

"We have no relationship, Billy. He simply asked if he could call on me. He says he has feelings for me and I feel tender toward him."

"What should I do?" Billy asked. "I'm charged with protecting your best interests. Is his heart true?"

Seesoff thought for a moment. "I'll have to find his truth when we are together. Is this fair in your eyes, my son?"

Billy looked at Seesoff, brows knitted over tired-looking eyes. "If this is what you want, I will accept it. If he mistreats you, I will hurt him."

"Thank you, Billy, I will be careful. He will need to come to you and explain his intentions. That is reasonable under your charge to protect me."

Charlee was happy to hear that Billy had agreed to allow Trae to see Seesoff. Billy had gone to her and explained what had happened. "I suppose some young fellow will be coming to me about seeing Star. That will be easier because she is clearly not ready for it."

They needed to go up to the Johnson ranch to see Ann.

Billy had collected a large amount of vegetables and fruit from neighboring ranches. Duane had ordered a supply of dried fruit and canned fruits and vegetables from his suppliers.

Billy hired two Indians to come along to the ranch to dig a new latrine pit. Charlee, Seesoff, and Billy took a light freight wagon with a brace of strong horses to haul the load.

The autumn day was cool and blustery. They arrived at the ranch midmorning. Ann sat on the porch and rose to wave when they drew up to the house. Billy unhitched the horses and led them around to the back. Calvin was out on the ranch checking his cattle.

Ann hugged Charlee and Seesoff as they stepped onto the porch. Elisabeth came out of the house looking fresher than before. Charlee had brought toothbrushes and tooth cleaning powder for the family. She walked Ann into the house to the sink. She gave Ann a red brush and showed her how to use it. Ann found pleasure in brushing her teeth. She said, "This feels nice but it hurts a little."

Charlee examined Ann. She seemed better, with more strength and vitality. Charlee noticed some dirt on Ann's hands, arms, and legs. "Elisabeth, we need to keep her clean. Come on, Ann, let's get in the tub." Seesoff started the bath as Charlee took Elisabeth outside to talk. "How is your family doing, Elisabeth?"

"We're much better, thank you. The food you brought has been greatly appreciated. We're all stronger."

The family's progress pleased Charlee. She had brought some apple juice along for them to drink.

"This drink will help your bowels and the scurvy. Let's go around and see how the men are doing." The men were busy digging the new pit. Billy had hooked the horses on the latrine skids and dragged it off the old pit. He poured lime on the residue and covered the hole with dirt. He planned to put a log over the dirt to mark the old hole.

When the new hole was finished they would attach the harness to a long rope and pull the latrine shed over the new hole. The shed would be cleaned inside with disinfectant.

Charlee and Elisabeth went around to the side of the house. They looked at the wagonload so Elisabeth could see what they had brought. Elisabeth was pleased. "We will have to put most of this in the root cellar. There is a small shed at the end of the porch." Three hours later the latrine was finished. The supplies were stored in the root cellar and the porch shed.

Billy talked about the ranch when Calvin came in. They made some agreements. They were going to meet in a few days at Murphy's to sign contracts.

All was well with the group as they left the ranch. Billy paid the Indians with coin and they rode off toward the camp. Charlee, Seesoff, and Billy were tired as they drove toward the settlement. It was dusk when they arrived.

Charlee found a note that a rancher wanted her to look at his arm. He would be back the next day. Billy had gone over to Murphy's to see Duane and Mildred. He told Duane about his talk with Calvin and the contracts that would be needed. Billy would draw up the contracts for Duane to examine.

"Billy," Mildred said as she ushered him into the kitchen for some coffee. "Trae Smith was in to see you. He seemed a little irritated. What's wrong?"

Billy told Mildred about the situation with Seesoff. Duane drifted in from the store. He had heard the part about Seesoff. "You had better be careful Billy. Trae went over to Pike's and is still there."

Billy groaned, "All I need now is a lovesick man who is mad at me. I'm tired. I'm going over to get Charlee and Seesoff for dinner. We'll wash up and be back soon."

Billy walked to the clinic to see the women. Star came in from her room and gave Billy a kiss on the cheek and a hug.

"How are you, little sister? Did you have a good day?" Charlee smiled and chirped in, "Your little sister is a beautiful woman. You will have to deal with the men coming calling on Star."

"Oh, not too soon, I hope," said Billy. He told them about Trae being in town.

They were sharing news about their trip to the Johnsons' place when Trae barged in the front door, huffing mad.

"Billy True," he said, lurching toward the group, "no man can tell me who I can and can't see."

"Back off, Trae," Billy said. "No reason for you to act this way."

Trae charged at Billy, swinging his fists trying to hit him. Billy moved to his left and whip-kicked Trae behind his left knee. Trae fell to the floor on his face. Billy stepped on Trae's left leg behind the knee and grabbed his foot with the left hand. He bent the leg over his foot and Trae screamed in pain. Billy grabbed Trae around the throat with his right arm and held him in a chokehold.

Billy had Trae in a painful hold. Trae was screaming in pain. Billy clinched up on the hold, rendering Trae helpless and protesting in pain. Seesoff stepped forward, put her arms around Billy's shoulders and said, "Please, Billy, don't hurt him any more, I care for him." Billy released his hold and stepped back.

He looked at Seesoff and said, "I didn't want this." He walked over to Charlee. "You and Seesoff better stay and take care of him. I'm going over to Murphy's and eat. I'll see you later." Billy left without another word.

Charlee and Seesoff helped Trae to the table. Charlee examined Trae's knee. "You have a severe sprain. Some ligaments may be involved. It will take some time to heal."

Trae, with some relief from the pain, said, "He's like a wildcat. I don't know what happened."

With a sad voice, Seesoff said, "Foolish man. Billy is the most dangerous man in the territory. He had you in an Apache chokehold. He could have killed you easily. You tested the warrior in him. There is much for you to do to make it up to him. You go home and come back to see me another day. I will talk to Billy to try and ease his anger."

# Chapter 17: Billy Helps Trae

Trae was confined to his house by the knee injury from the fight with Billy. Seesoff and Charlee rode up to see him and examine the knee. Trae was in pain so Charlee gave him laudanum to take in small doses. They talked about the problem with Billy and the relationship between Trae and Seesoff.

"Billy is a kind man," Charlee said. "People don't know him. You attacked and the warrior spirit in him came out."

Trae grinned. "I hate to think of what would have happened to me if he were a bad man."

"I told you not to test him, Trae," Charlee continued without smiling. "He scares me sometimes with his ability to do damage. You should see him on the shooting range. He can draw and fire before other men clear the holster. I draw against him on the range. He plays with me and fires two rounds before I can even shoot." She lightened her tone. "How are things going, Trae?"

"I'm feeling better. I can't do much. A darned cat came down and killed one of my cows. He ate part of it and left the rest. Those cats can be a real problem."

"Would you like me to ask Billy to come and try to get the cat?" Charlee asked.

"I don't know. Do you think he would?"

"He often helps ranchers with rogue bears and cats. I'll ask him if he'll come."

When the women returned to the settlement, Charlee went to see Billy. He was in the store working on contracts for Calvin Johnson.

"Billy, can I talk to you?"

"Sure can." He kissed and hugged her, lifting her off the ground. "What can I do for you?"

"We were up to see Trae today. He'll be hobbled for a while. A cat's coming down close to his ranch and has killed a cow. Could you go up and try to get him?"

Billy's mood turned somber. "Isn't that asking a lot of me, Charlee? He attacks me and now you want me to help him."

"Billy, you're greater than other men in just about every way. I'm asking you to be great in your forgiveness."

"You're laying it on a little thick, aren't you, Charlee?" Billy said with a smile.

"Maybe so, but it's true. People expect more of you than other men." She came close and put her forehead on Billy's jaw. "I love you." She playfully danced away.

"You don't leave me much choice. You sure know how to work me. I'll get ready and go up today."

Billy went over to the kitchen and asked Mildred if he could have some jerky and biscuits. She was startled and concerned. "Is this going to be a dangerous thing you're doing?"

"No, I'm going up to try to get a cat that's killing cattle on Trae Smith's place."

"Trae Smith? That's a surprise."

"Charlee talked me into it," Billy said.

Billy checked his Sharps, loaded it, and carried his rig over to the corral to saddle a horse. He was on his way in a few minutes. Down the road he realized he had forgotten his food. He would have to do without and hope the hunt was not long.

He was riding along at a walk when he heard a call. He turned to see Charlee laid over her horse, riding bareback at a full gallop. What a rider she is, Billy thought. She reined in along side of him and handed him a sack of jerky and biscuits. "You're getting a little careless, aren't you, Scout?" Charlee said.

"Not as long as I have you to back me up, Charlee." Billy took the opportunity to lean over and give her a big kiss.

"Thank you, Billy. I'll see you tonight. Have a good hunt." Charlee rode away toward the settlement.

Billy rode to Trae's ranch house and stepped off his horse. He walked up to the door and knocked. Trae came limping out and with surprise in his eyes said hello to Billy.

"Trae, I'm up to try and get the cat."

"Thanks, Billy. Come in and have a cup of coffee."

Billy moved through the door into a small kitchen that opened up into a large family room. They sat at a table and Trae poured a strong cup of coffee.

"Sorry about your leg, Trae," Billy said.

"It was a dumb thing for me to do. Fighting is one thing, fighting with you is foolish."

"I wish I wouldn't have tightened down on the hold. It wouldn't have hurt you so much."

"Billy, I understand you could have killed me easily. I'm ahead of the game. About Seesoff, can I call on her?"

Billy paused then said, "If it is okay with her, you have my permission. If you hurt her, I may kill you next time."

They shook hands and Billy got up to leave. "This cat was here three days ago. I might catch him coming back over his pattern. He may be staying around because young cattle are easy to kill. I'll find his trail and try to read his pattern, then I'll find a place to lie and wait for him."

Billy rode up from the house and found the remains of the last kill. The cat had fed twice on this kill. He might come back or could look for a fresh kill.

He followed the cat's trail and found where it had repeated paths. Billy found good grass nearby in an open area and hobbled his horse. He was downwind from his horse. The animal would be bait. Billy could also watch the cat's crosstrails.

He found a vantage point and walked up to post himself. Suddenly, fifteen yards ahead of him, a large brown bear rose up. The bear had been feeding on berries, but it growled and snarled when it caught Billy's scent. He'd been careless; his senses had not told him the bear was near.

Billy cocked the hammer of his Sharps, ready to fire. He raised the gun high above his head in both hands, so that he appeared about eight feet tall. "Brother Bear, I don't have business with you today." In a loud voice he shouted and growled furiously. The bear turned and rumbled off through the brush. He looked back often to see if this animal was after him.

Billy lowered his gun and closed the hammer. He could have killed the bear if needed. He went to his chosen vantage point and settled in. He scanned the area with his glass. There was nothing but the usual ground animals. Black-tailed jackrabbits and ground squirrels darted about in the brush.

Mourning doves passed through in rapid flight.

Billy leaned up against a rock and scanned the surrounding area. He needed to spend more time in the mountains watching and listening. He was losing his keen senses. The senses of sound and smell were dull or the bear would not have surprised him. He should have smelled the bear and heard the foraging for berries. Yes, he thought, I need more time out in these places. I need to listen to the gods of nature and use the skills I've been taught. He looked up at the sky and made a silent promise to ride and camp more, to listen to nature's voice.

Evening was approaching. He drank some water and ate biscuits and jerky. Thanks to Charlee, he thought. His mind drifted to her. Soon he would be her husband and she would be his wife.

It was there, then, faint movement in the brush alongside the grass where his horse was hobbled. The horse sounded an alarm of fright. The shot would be a hundred yards, Billy estimated. Billy set his sights on the Sharps and rested his arm on his knee to steady his hold. He watched the mountain lion stalk along the brush next to the grass. Billy sighted and fired. The impact of the .50 caliber bullet bowled the cat over. The animal kicked for a few seconds, then lay still. The horse pranced about, neighing and whinnying in alarm. Billy reloaded his Sharps and walked down to calm his horse.

Billy settled the horse and went to where the cat lay. He estimated the cat to be about six feet long from nose to the tip of the tail. An average sized cat, at about 125 pounds. Billy pulled back the still-warm lips and examined the teeth. The cat was old. This might explain why he was killing cattle to eat. A healthy cat in his prime kills deer and avoids approaching man and his cattle. Billy ran his hand along the animal's flank. I hope you fathered many cubs, he told the animal silently. Billy cut off the cat's ears to show Trae. He left the body for the disposal of nature by other hungry creatures.

Trae was pleased when Billy came in and told him about the hunt. Billy gave Trae the ears of the cat and rushed off to get back to Charlee.

Billy's new attitude relieved Trae. He was well aware of Billy's commitment to Seesoff. If he mistreated her, Billy would be there to make him pay consequences. Billy could be a good friend, but Trae knew better than to cross him. Trae had never feared a man until he met this young scout.

# Chapter 18: The House

Charlee and Billy hitched up the buckboard and headed out to see the house. It was a lazy October day, crisp but warm. They enjoyed the trotting pace. Fluffy clouds rolled by. The sycamores and chokecherry trees were still rich in character around the streams.

The couple was just short of the turnoff to the house when they met three young riders on the road. Billy said "Hi, boys" as he drew up the horse.

"Hold on, who's the honey with you?"

Billy was ready to respond when Charlee touched his arm and said, "A little more respect would be in order, men. Is this the way you treat ladies where you come from?"

"Well, if your man's going to let you do the talking, we don't know if you're a lady, do we?" one man said with a laugh. The others jibbed in.

Charlee's Colt was out in a flash and she fired two shots in the ground between their horses. The animals jumped and bucked as the riders cursed and struggled to keep control.

"I said a little respect was in order."

The men were furious as their horses settled down. "What are you doing, lady?" the mouthy one said.

Billy warned, "She could shoot your ears off, boys. Let's settle down. I'm the constable here. What brings you in?"

The men looked at Charlee and grinned sheepishly. She still had her Colt leveled at them. One man said, "I'm coming in to get some help. I have a tooth that's killing me. We understand there is someone here who could help."

Billy and Charlee passed a look. "That's possible," Billy said. "She won't be in the settlement for a couple of hours. You go on in and behave yourselves."

"You boys are lucky my man didn't have to deal with this. It would have been much worse for you."

"Why is that?" one man muttered.

Charlee crowed, "This is Billy True and he would shoot your ears off, and some other parts too if he wanted."

Her words sent a chill through the men and they moved around the wagon and went forward toward the settlement.

Billy laughed as he made the turn up to the house. The workers were busy around the place as the wagon pulled up in front. "This is going to be a nice place for us, Charlee."

The cement foundation was poured. The framing was up. The outside wall-covering of one-inch planking was on. The walls were eight-inches thick with adobe bricks between the inside and outside walls. The inside wall was smoothed one-inch planking. The walls would make for warmth in the winter and coolness in the summer. They were good for defense with appropriate gun ports.

Planking floors glowed throughout. Drainage was installed for inside plumbing. The flushing toilet they had heard about from travelers from the East was still new technology and not trustworthy. Instead, the couple chose an outside latrine with an elevated plank walkway.

A large covered porch ran alongside the front of the house. The floor plan was rectangular with the long side to the front. A large room with a wood-burning stove adjoined the kitchen. The cast iron stove was new to the frontier and replaced the inefficient fireplace. Billy imagined sitting there on winter evenings with Charlee.

A door in the great room entered a hallway leading to four bedrooms. The hallway ended at the back porch, which was enclosed and served as a mudroom and entry. An outside door led to the latrine walkway.

The roof was a one-inch planking base. This was framed by two-inch framing crisscrossed over the base planking. The framing was filled with a layer of adobe mud. This layer was covered with overlapped one-inch planking and sealed with peat pitch. Trusses resting on log beams supported the roof. Stripped and finished log posts underpinned the beams.

Charlee and Billy walked around and through the house. Charlee had made all of her changes and the house was nearing completion.

They viewed the surrounding area. Pine trees ringed the house on two sides. The south side opened to pasture. The front opened to the road. Billy wanted at least a one-hundred-yard clearance around the house for defense purposes.

The couple was satisfied with the house and their hearts were glad as they left for the settlement. Both were lost in thought and time flew. In a short time they arrived at the settlement stables. After he settled the wagon and horses, Billy and Charlee walked arm-in-arm to the clinic.

They entered the clinic and found three men in hot discussion with Seesoff. "These men want to see you, Charlee," Seesoff said as she hastily left the room. The men were startled to see the gun-toting girl from the road.

Charlee said, "I'm a nurse and will try to help you."

"What's that Indian doing here?"

Billy stepped forward, "Watch your mouth. I want no trouble here. She is Charlee's assistant and my Indian mother. Let it go or leave."

The man with the bad tooth grimaced in pain and said, "I don't want trouble. Can you fix this tooth?"

"I don't know. Let me look at it." She washed her hands and asked the man to lie on the table. She cranked the table up to form a backrest.

"Open your mouth, please." The man groaned as Charlee probed around his tooth and gums. She felt his jaw and neck and found no nodes that would indicate infection. The gums around the tooth were red and swollen.

"Seesoff, would you get me a sharp probe and sterilize it with alcohol?"

"Is this going to hurt?" asked the man.

"Not too badly, I hope."

Charlee took the probe from Seesoff and started feeling between the gum and tooth. The gums bled as she removed debris. She found various particles, seeds from foods, and a kernel from popcorn. She cleaned the gums around the entire tooth.

"That is your problem," said Charlee. "Those things under your gums were irritating the tissue. You have been parking your chew there too. That's not good. Stop chewing that slop, or at least keep it away from the sore area. You don't seem to have decay yet."

Charlee went over to the storage cabinet and got a toothbrush. "Use this brush everyday with baking soda. Rinse with diluted vinegar or some whiskey. Take better care of your teeth or you will be in to see me about pulling a tooth."

The man's pain had subsided considerably. "How much do I owe you, Miss Charlee?"

"Two dollars, unless you can't afford it."

The man collected from his friends and they came up with two dollars.

Charlee, Seesoff, and Billy laughed as the men left and walked to their horses. Billy said, "They will remember the day when a beautiful, gun-toting nurse fixed a tooth."

Charlee gazed at her true love and her dear friend, one on either side of her, and said, "As our lives go by we will see many wonders. Life is good when I have family, friends, and my Billy."

# Chapter 19: The Wedding

In the next several weeks Charlee spent much time out at the ranch planning the wedding with Bertha and Willard. They reminisced about Charlee's childhood. As a little girl with no siblings to play with, Charlee had found fun in the opportunities the ranch offered.

Willard reminded Charlee she had been a strong girl. She could blend in with the ranch hands and pull her weight. She was riding the range with Willard when she was five. At seven, she started roping calves. By ten, Charlee was firing rifles and pistols with her dad.

Charlee was equally at home in the kitchen, her mom told her. She took her role as a ranch woman seriously. They teased her about early kitchen setbacks. Her first yellow cake fell seconds after she pulled it from the oven. In disgust, she fed it to the chickens; they thought it was just fine. By the time Charlee was twelve, she could manage the kitchen alone. She and her mother developed a rhythm in the kitchen and could cook enough food for a work crew of fifty men without a wrinkle.

Bertha and Willard were good tutors, letting their daughter explore. Charlee was a powerhouse of a girl. She'd always had her opinions and people learned to respect them. She wasn't just a girl, she was a ranch hand and ranch woman rolled into one. She fought against dresses and skirts, favoring pants. She was straddle riding from the start and never touched a sidesaddle.

Charlee was also a beauty. She kept herself perked up and could fit in a parlor activity with the ladies without a thought. At a moment she could sit down with the boys to play a mean hand of poker.

When Charlee first met Billy, he was just thirteen. He treated her with respect and consideration. As a young girl would, she thought he was a god. He would ride in wearing buckskins and packing a Colt. He could do a hard day's work and would be happy with a nice meal and conversation.

When Charlee reached thirteen, her parents knew she loved Billy as more than a pal. Overwhelmed, Billy worked hard to ward off her intensity. She would overpower his feelings at times. He would retreat into the mountains so his mind could clear, and he could tune his senses.

Charlee and Billy seemed ordained to be together. Each had a strong personal aura. Their auras would blend into one without losing individual strength. They were two magnificent people, destined to leave their marks on others and their impact on the territory.

The wedding was to be a modest affair. It would not be embellished with elaborate decorations and activities. Clay Sprague's father was a self-styled preacher in the area and would officiate at the ceremony. Duane, the justice of the peace, would sign the certificate of matrimony. He would also be Billy's best man.

The November weather could potentially present a problem so the ceremony was to be in the recreation hall. The reception was planned on the south side of Murphy's. A one-quarter beef would be on the spit at the southeast corner of the store, and a plank dance floor would be laid. A group of ranch people planned to provide music with guitar, violin, accordion, and harmonica.

Mildred was in charge of the food. Star and Seesoff would help in the preparation and presentation. Bertha was in charge of preparing for the ceremony. Seesoff would be the maid of honor no matter who thought what of her presence there. "Send them to me," Charlee said whenever Seesoff or Star reported cruelties from passersby.

Billy assisted wherever he could. He made regular visits to the shooting range. His skill as a gunfighter could be tested at any time. One morning Billy was in Murphy's working at the gun bench. Duane came in with a package that had been delivered by courier the day before. A courier usually did not carry a package of this size. It was marked special handling.

"What do you think it is, Dad?"

"I don't know. Let's get it opened and see."

The package was well padded and housed in a strong box. Opening the box, Billy was startled by the display of two black Colts. He lifted them out and tested their heft and balance. "I've never felt a gun this nice. Good balance. It doesn't drift up and down in my hold. It's heavy enough to handle the recoil, but not too heavy."

He was examining one gun and on the barrel he noticed an engraving, which said, "Billy True Lightning." He checked the other: the same. He wondered if this was going to be another line of gun or just personalized for him.

Billy took the guns over to show Charlee. She and Seesoff

were washing the floors of the clinic. When Charlee saw the guns she squealed and said, "Let's go shoot them, Billy." They left the clinic and went over to the store to get ammunition.

"Dad, I need to get a cross-over holster for my longer gun. When I'm on the prowl now, I'll carry two holstered guns."

"We have some in stock. You will have to choose one and rub it with leather oil to shape it to the gun."

"I'll do that, starting today. Charlee and I are going to the range to shoot. I'll need some ammunition. You can take a turn with the guns later."

Charlee and Billy walked up to the range. They staked up their targets. Billy took the first turn on both guns. The .44/40 Colts were smooth shooting in his hands. He drew and fired several times on both guns. He worked with Charlee on her draw and firing. She was smooth and accurate.

"I'm pretty good with these guns, Billy. Seeing them used in your hands is scary. The name 'Lightning' is appropriate when you use them."

Billy and Charlee needed to ride out to the Darrow ranch to make some final wedding plans. They wanted an opportunity for Billy to make peace with the Darrows, particularly Bertha. They took the buckboard to have a nice drive. Along the way, they stopped by the cemetery to visit Molly's grave and lay greenery and flowers around her headstone.

It was a cloudy day, cool and blustery. They encountered scores of madrone trees with their distinctive reddish bark. A few large cypress trees grew up the canyons near creeks. Noisy woodpeckers worked around the cottonwoods, hunting insects and socializing.

Billy had brought his new Colts to show Willard. He

thought it would be a good topic of conversation to start with. They pulled into the familiar road leading to the house. Billy recalled it looked the same as he first time he had seen it many years ago.

He and Charlee had grown up together on the ranch. They rode with Willard on trips into the hills. Billy showed her the many animal tracks and the stories they told, a bobcat chasing a rabbit or a pack of coyotes on the hunt.

Charlee would take Billy into the kitchen to share some cookies or rolls she had baked. She was spinning her web, but Billy didn't know it. Charming as a young girl, she quickly grew into a woman right in front of Billy and the world.

They pulled up in front of the house and Billy tied the horses to a hitching post. Charlee greeted her parents with hugs. Billy went forward and shook hands with Willard and gave Bertha a respectful embrace.

As the day progressed the barriers in relationships melted away like ice after a thaw. Billy and Bertha were jovial and playful.

The wedding plans were almost complete for a ceremony that promised to be plain but meaningful. Charlee invited Claw Hand, her Indian father. She smiled to think Claw Hand would wonder why Billy was marrying Charlee again. She had been introduced as Billy's wife. She would have to explain this to him some day.

After easy good-byes with the Darrows, the young couple left the ranch and drove home, arriving at dusk. It had been a good day for them. Billy felt more at peace with the Darrows.

They drove into the stables to put the horses and rig away. Murphy's was a welcome sight. They found two young men sitting in Murphy's talking to Star. Billy approached them and said, "Did you get permission to socialize with Star?"

"Yes, sir, Mr. Murphy said we could if he supervised."

Star came up to Billy, "Billy, they are just young friends my age. I see no harm."

"If they asked permission and you were supervised, I guess it's okay."

Billy walked over to Duane. "I guess that's all we can do. Star is going go give us some grief. She is such a pretty girl. Bees will come to honey."

Charlee had gone to the clinic. She and Seesoff discussed a patient who was waiting. The woman was near to delivery time, but Charlee had not seen her for prenatal care. They were concerned where she would deliver. The woman, whose name was Jessie, had come down because she thought she felt contractions. This was her first child.

Jessie lived on a small ranch, where her husband had stayed behind. She was facing the childbirth alone. Charlee was angry with the husband for not coming down with her.

"Billy," Charlee called when she saw him outside, "Would you go up to Jessie Young's ranch and get her husband here? She is showing signs of delivery."

"What if he doesn't want to come?"

"You tell him I'll come up and pistol whip him," Charlee said. Then she smiled. "You'll persuade him, Billy. Please hurry." She added, "I get a little tired of this cavalier attitude some men have about this time in a woman's life. The woman will work hard up to and after the delivery, often with very little rest." Charlee was intent on making this point.

Charlee called to Seesoff, "I'll start getting Jessie ready for delivery. You wash down the table and attach the stirrups."

Charlee had to wash Jessie thoroughly to help prevent infection. She comforted the young woman as much as possible. "I delivered several babies in Prescott. We will do this together, Jessie." She tucked Jessie in with a warm blanket.

Possible complications worried Charlee but she showed only confidence in front of her patient. I have assisted on cesarean sections at Prescott and have all the equipment, she told herself as she felt the woman's abdomen with her strong hands. Privately, she informed Seesoff they would have to look for a breech position of the baby. Other complications might be a narrow pelvis, cervical obstruction, or the mother's exhaustion.

Billy approached the Young ranch at almost dark. He found Clyde Young putting away his horses after tilling soil.

"Clyde, could I talk to you?" Billy slid off his horse and moved toward Clyde.

"Hold on there, who are you?" Clyde said with some alarm.

"I'm Billy True, from the settlement. Your wife is about ready to deliver your baby. Charlee wants you to come down and help by giving Jessie comfort."

"Comfort! She's a ranch wife, she doesn't need comfort." Clyde stiffened up.

"Clyde, she's young and scared. This is her first child." He saw Clyde's deep frown and changed tactics. "Don't you want to see your baby?"

"Never thought too much about it," Clyde remarked as he sized Billy up.

"Clyde, I would appreciate it if you would come along." He acted sheepish. "Truth is, I'll be in trouble with my own woman if you don't come." Billy saw a shift in the man.

"Did you say Jessie was scared?"

"Yes, she is."

"I'll get my horse and come along." Over his shoulder he

said, "I just realized who you are."

"Hey, I didn't put any muscle on you," Billy assured him. "I think you want to come anyway."

Clyde shrugged.

Billy and Clyde rode out at a gallop. Clyde was bareback on his horse, not taking time to saddle up. The settlement was not far away and they would be there shortly.

On the table, Jessie cried from labor pains. Charlee read the dilation. Things looked good. Billy and Clyde rode up and entered the clinic. Charlee grabbed Clyde and took him to the sink to wash his hands and arms. She put a surgical apron on him and they marched into the delivery room. Jessie cried for joy when she saw Clyde. He shed a tear, too.

To Charlee's relief, the baby's birth came easily. Once, Charlee had to move its shoulder a little to ease the delivery, but the baby boy looked healthy. Charlee severed the umbilical cord and delivered the afterbirth.

Seesoff cleaned the child of blood and residue from the birth. She cuddled the baby in a blanket and placed him on Jessie's chest. A new life had come into the territory.

The day before the wedding Billy and Charlee went to the range to shoot. They worked with Billy's Lightning Colts and Charlee's regular Peacemaker Colt.

When they arrived back at Murphy's they were surprised to see Mark Evans and Al Sieber having lunch. Both had heard of the wedding and made long trips to come. Mark came from Prescott with regards from General Crook. Al Sieber came from San Carlos with regards from John Clum, the Indian agent.

Both had other motives, too. Mark wanted to see Star. Al wanted to talk to Billy about mining in the area as an investment.

Charlee was intentionally reserved as she shook hands with Mark.

Al said, "Billy where did you find this jewel?"

Charlee, with a little bow said, "Thank you, sir."

Billy was anxious to show the men his new Colts. The guns impressed them and clearly aroused their envy.

"I have been scouting for many years and been wounded several times," Al said. "No one ever gave me a special gun."

"You're so old and ugly," Mark joked, "who would want to make a hero out of you?"

Al chuckled. "You're right about that."

Charlee interrupted, "Would you men like something cold to drink? We have tea, lemonade, beer, and hard liquor if you like."

They opted for lemonade. Al was rumored to be a heavy drinker, but those stories were exaggerated. Mark limited himself to wine with meals. Billy didn't drink alcohol. He kept his senses clear at all times.

They talked about scouting in the territory. Al advised Billy to stop point-scouting and go to the method of scouting units. Al was using trained Apache scouts as fighting units operating in front of the cavalry. This was very effective and more secure.

Charlee was excited. "Billy, listen to Mr. Sieber. He has given you a strategy to use in your scouting. This could keep you safer and still be effective."

Al and Mark were tired from traveling and needed some rest. Billy said, "Your stay is on me. The hotel is clean and the food is good. It is an honor to have you for the wedding."

Al went to check into the hotel. Mildred was pleased to have such a famous person stay at her place.

Mark wanted to talk to Billy. "Billy, I would like to see Star while I'm here. I know how you feel. My intentions are honorable and I give my assurances as an officer."

Billy had become more lenient with Star in these matters. "It will be acceptable for you to be with her as long as you acknowledge that she is young and inexperienced. Try not to worry me by wandering off alone." Billy shook Mark's hand and smiled, saying, "This guardian role is getting to be harder with both of the women involved."

Charlee came by and said, "Billy, there are some details we need to discuss about the wedding. Things seem to be ready, but I'm getting a little nervous."

"I'm a little edgy myself." Billy said. "I look forward to when it's all over, to being with you in our house, sitting on the porch."

As they walked along the street, they could see the wedding preparations developing. Chairs and benches were lined up in the recreation hall. Colorful papier-mâché and crepe paper added texture to the hall's drab walls.

The shelves and cabinets were moved together at Murphy's to allow for the seating and gathering of people. The weather might demand inside activities. The south side of Murphy's was ready with the dance floor down. There was seating of planks and cement blocks.

Mildred and Bertha were busy in the kitchen getting food ready to be cooked. The seasoned meat was hanging in the cool pantry. Star and Seesoff had been decorating the area. When Mark came to see Star, he was drafted to help with the decorations. Billy smiled to see Mark holding a pile of tablecloths for Star. That evening all of those who helped with preparations joined together at a huge feast. The event brought unity to the settlement.

Charlee woke up slowly the next day. She sat in the

window of her room, letting her thoughts drift like leaves floating in a stream. The day had come. The wedding was scheduled for one o'clock in the afternoon.

Chairs, people, flowers, food, and decorations filled the recreation hall. Aisles were left open for the procession. Billy was in his suit, with a handkerchief in his lapel. A small Colt revolver was in the inside pocket of his coat. Duane wore a dark suit.

They went down the aisle and stood with Mr. Sprague. To the side stood Claw Hand, dressed in his fine feathery. Much to the surprise of everyone, the shaman was there. Bertha and Mildred had been seated in front.

The women wore full-length cotton dresses of pale yellow and cream with flowing skirts. Hand-embroidered roses embellished the fitted bodices. A simple veil covered Charlee's face.

Musicians played as the procession started down the aisle. The sight of Charlee took Billy's breath away. Willard and Charlee approached the front.

Mr. Sprague asked, "Who gives this bride away?"

"I do," said Willard as he handed Charlee over to Billy. Seesoff and Duane came alongside the couple. Sprague cleared his throat.

"We are here to bind these young people together in holy matrimony. If anyone believes they shouldn't be married, speak now." He allowed a moment of silence as he glared around the hall.

"Charlee and Billy, you have consented to be together, for better or worse, for the rest of your lives. You shall not part until one of you dies. Charlee you must honor and obey Billy, and Billy you must honor, respect, and protect Charlee. Do you understand this?"

"Yes." They spoke in unison.

"Billy, do you take Charlee to be your wife?"

"Yes, I do," said Billy.

"Do you, Charlee, take Billy as your husband?"

"Yes, I do," said Charlee.

Sprague stepped aside and said, "I understand Chief Claw Hand will say something?"

Claw Hand nodded. "White Fawn and White Warrior," he addressed the couple, "my blessing is for you to move happily through the seasons of life. The seasons of 'Many Leaves,' 'Ghost Faces of Winter,' and 'Thick with Fruit.'" He stepped forward and placed his hands on their heads. "Bless you, and may the gods give you many sons and daughters."

Claw Hand stepped back and made way for the shaman. The old man came forward slowly and placed the couple's hands on a feather-decorated cane. "This cane will absorb the power of this ceremony. Keep it for the rest of your lives and keep your vows." He moved back in his place.

Sprague stepped forward. "With the power vested from all of us, I now pronounce you man and wife. You can kiss her now, Billy."

Billy raised Charlee's veil and kissed her respectfully on the mouth. "I love you, Charlee."

Charlee clung close. "I have wanted this ever since I was a little girl." She rose up on her toes and gave Billy a long kiss, to the delight and applause from the crowd. Bertha looked around at the cheering gathering.

The procession moved out of the hall and down to Murphy's for refreshments and dancing. Charlee and Billy circulated through the crowd, receiving congratulations. Several hours later, Charlee and Billy went to their rooms to change clothes.

They came out wearing denim clothes and sporting Colts. They planned to go to their unfinished house and stay for two days. The workmen were asked to work half days in the afternoon so Billy and Charlee would have more private time.

They said their good-byes and loaded the buckboard with clothes and supplies. They were surprised by a large group of people tying buckets and cans on the back of the buggy. A driver took over for Billy and they all followed, banging pans and other noisemakers. They went up and down the street giving the couple an enthusiastic shivaree. It was all in good fun and was a fine salute to the pair.

Billy and Charlee spent two days in a sublime state. They were together in the ways they had longed for.

Three months later the Ghost Face of winter was on the land. They were in their new house and sat bundled up on the porch swing, talking of their future. Charlee said, "Billy, I think I have little Luke inside me."

"Or maybe Piper Rae," Billy said as he squeezed Charlee closer.

Their future was going to be challenging but bright: two exceptional people in demanding times. They had faced the many challenges of the frontier, Charlee the healer and Billy the strong-arm of security and order. They were partners in a violent land, helping the settlement, and growing into people who would leave a mark on the history of the territory.

# Glossary

**.44 Colt**  The Colt is the make of a handgun Billy used. The caliber of the gun is .44. It was a six-shot revolver, single action. It was the most popular gun of the time.

**"brows" of a mountain**  A landscape feature describing the projecting upper part or edge of a steep place.

**Al Sieber**  Born in Germany, he served in the Civil War with honor. He moved to Prescott in 1865 and became chief of scouts for General George Crook and served with distinction in the Tonto Basin Campaign of 1872–1873. He earned the respect of the Indians. He was accidentally killed in 1907 working on the Roosevelt Dam.

**Apache chokehold**  Billy learned many holds while training with the Apaches. He made variations on them as he grew older. He was always prepared for action by being clearheaded.

**bigheaded**  The term Indians used to describe the stubborn attitude White doctors had toward Indian medicine.

**bivouac area**  This is an encampment with little or no shelter, used for a short time.

**breaks**    Breaks are a line of cliffs, spurs, and small ravines at the edge of a mountain.

**breech-loading**    In a breech-loading weapon, the shell goes in at the rear of the bore. A lever closes a breechblock against the force of the charge.

**buckskins**    Garments made from the skin of a deer, they were generally soft and pliable. Some expensive types were suede-finished skins.

**Buckskin Hat**    He was one of the main Apache war chiefs that fought General Crook's army in the war of 1872–1873.

**buffalo soldiers**    The name given to Black cavalry soldiers by the Indians.

**carbolic acid**    British surgeon Joseph Lister discovered the use of antiseptics in 1867. He used carbolic acid to prevent infection.

**commode**    A chamber pot or toilet used inside, then emptied in the outside latrine; used mainly at night or with sick people who are unable to use the latrine.

**cracker barrel**    On the frontier, many stores had barrels filled with crackers for people to snack on as they sat around and talked.

**draw**    A draw is a shallow gully in the land.

**draw down**    This means to pull your gun for use.

**feather-decorated cane**    The feathered cane was used in many ceremonies. One purpose was to absorb evil spirits.

**field-dressed**    Cleaning a deer or other animal where it was killed. This generally includes removing the entrails and certain glands.

**four up and six up**    Four or six horses pulling a rig.

**Geronimo**    Last of the great Apache chiefs, he waged war against the United States Army until 1886. He was captured and shipped to Florida with his followers. He died in 1909.

**gritty**   Being persistent, courageous, or in this case, foolish and irritating.

**healed**   Describes a man carrying a gun.

**hogback**   This is a ridge of land with a sharp summit and steeply slopping sides.

**honey bucket**   A crude name for a bucket used as a toilet.

**hurrah**   This term was used to describe when cowboys and others came into a town to celebrate and make trouble.

**John Clum**   He was appointed Indian agent at San Carlos in 1874. He respected the Apache and was an outspoken critic of the military and its treatment of the Indians.

**Lyman Bridges Company**   A leading prefabrication plant that shipped structures to the West.

**Mazatzal Mountains**   This range of mountains runs about fifty miles along the west side of the valley where the settlement is located.

**Mogollon Rim**   A range of mountains running east and west along the Tonto Basin, it is about 100 miles long and has peaks up to 10,000 feet. The southern edge has jagged cliffs dropping down to 4,000 feet to the breaks.

**muscle**   This means to have enough power to back up your word.

**pattern**   A mountain lion has a territory and a pattern of movement to hunt the area.

**pommel bag**   Billy used this bag to carry extra equipment and a built-in holster for an extra gun. There were models of the pummel bag for other purposes.

**Prescott**   This town was the capital of the territory at this time. It was a key commerce center.

**raiding and warfare**   There was a distinct difference

between raiding and warfare. Raiding was to "search out enemy property." Warfare was to "take death from the enemy."

**San Carlos Reservation** This was land set aside for Apache Indians to live apart from the settlers. It was located eighty miles east of the settlement near Globe, Arizona.

**scabbard** This is a rifle case for protection and carriage. They first appeared in the 1830s among the Indians of the Great Plains. Usually made of leather, they were attached full saddle or with a saddle horn loop.

**shaman** This was a holy man and healer in the Apache culture. He was like a priest and second only to the chief in power.

**Sharps rifle** Billy carried the Sharps .50/70 military conversion rifle. It was a .50-caliber bullet size with 70 as the length of the casing in millimeters. The length of the casing determines the amount of powder used. The amount of powder determines the power of the bullet.

**shivaree** This is a mock serenade to celebrate newly married couples. It is a rural custom.

**squaw man** A White man who takes an Indian as his wife. The term is used with contempt.

**stand of deer** Deer occupying a place or location are called a stand.

**Tontos** Tontos were a tribe of Apache Indians known as good fighters, though some settled down to farm. There were Northern Tontos and Southern Tontos.

**Verde** This was a major military camp in 1865 set up to protect local communities. It was changed to a new location in 1868 and again in 1870. General Crook used Camp Verde in the 1872–1873 Tonto Basin war. Verde became a temporary reservation for the Apaches after the war.

**war club** This was made from an animal's hide wrapped around a hardwood stick. At the end was a rock sewn inside the skin. A thong of leather was attached to the other end to fit around the wrist.

**wickiup** The Apache used a house of sticks and brush called a *wickiup*. They also used teepees, as did the Plains Indians.

**Winchester '73** This was a popular gun. Billy's was a .44/40-caliber rifle. The rifle was a longer gun with good accuracy and range. The carbine was a shorter gun for easy use from a saddle scabbard.

**Winchester** This rifle or carbine was very popular.

**yahoo** An uncouth or rowdy person.

# Acknowledgments

I would like to acknowledge...

Sadie McClendon, my editor, who helped me through the editing process for book publication.

Tom McGuigan, past president of the North Gila Historical Society in Payson.AZ. He was very helpful in the research process.

Alexa Mergan, my consulting editor, who helped me through the many phases of preparing the manuscript for submission.

Lisa Kimble, journalist, for her assistance as a consulting publicist.

The staff of the Payson Museum for their gracious assistance during my visits to the area.

# The Little Book with the Big Story

Jack was born in Kansas, and came out of the drought and depression of the 1930's. During his school years he moved around, not staying more than a year in one place. In 1945 he attended high school in Bakersfield, CA, and was influenced dramatically by his coaches and teachers.

After high school, Jack saw action in the Korean War, serving with the Navy on patrol frigates off North Korea. After discharge from the service, he attended colleges receiving a B.A., M.A., and an Ed.D. He worked in the field of Special Education and was a Director of Special Education for twenty-seven years. He has been a Lecturer at the

University level, preparing teachers to work in Special Education.

During his life, Dr. Schuetz has been intrigued by the frontier life of the West and the challenge of outdoor experiences. He has spent years camping, backpacking, hunting, fishing and in nature study. Jack has acquired a large reference library for frontier life, Indians, cowboys, gunfighters and the American Indian wars.

# Endorsements

Jack Schuetz gives us a bird's-eye view of what life was like growing up in the 1860s and 1870s in a small settlement in Arizona. Mr. Schuetz weaves an exciting adventure story while managing the strong character development of Charlee Rae and Billy True as they go from childhood friends to adults who love one another.

—Mary Jo Buckle
Retired elementary school teacher
Bakersfield, California

This is a very entertaining story that captures the spirit of a time gone by. The historical and geographical accuracy that Jack Schuetz weaves throughout the book is commendable and not often found nor generally expected in fictional writings intended for adolescents.

—Bill Ketchum
Retired IBM Executive
Dodge Center, Minnesota

Billy and Charlee Rae and a cast of characters, some fictional and some real, jump at you out of the West the way it once was, keeping you interested while they chase outlaws, battle prejudice, and save a community. Yes, there is even romance.

—Tom McGuigan
Past President
Northern Gila County Historical Society
Payson, Arizona

This action-packed tale of a young man and woman facing the challenges of the Western Frontier delivers a strong moral message in words and setting that will excite readers. You will easily identify with the colorful characters while enjoying a vivid and accurate glimpse into the history of the Arizona Frontier.

—Bob Morrison
Retired School Principal
San Jose, California

I found *The Adventures of Charlee Rae and Billy True* to be an exciting adventure story having many historical facts about the Arizona Territory in the 1860s and 1870s.

—Richard B. Rhodes
Retired School Superintendent
Fresno, California

Jack Schuetz has captured the life and spirit of a young man and woman challenged by the harsh and awe-inspiring frontier of the Southwest. As Billy, the scout, faces growing up with outlaws, Indians, the wilderness, and a diverse extended family, you become inspired by his youthful wisdom and responsibility. Equally inspiring is the development of Charlee by her own spunk to become a frontier doctor. A love story that hits the target, cited in with historical terms as only an educator can make enjoyable.

—Bob Shore
CEO, winemaker, farmer and petroleum engineer
Paso Robles, California